CW00689237

The characters, premises, and events in this book are fictitious. Names, characters, and plots are a product of the author's imagination. Any similarity to real persons, living or dead, is coincidental and not intended by the author.

TABLE OF CONTENTS:

Second Time Around

'Hello!' Simon called out into the old barn building in Corbridge. The room was full of furniture at varying stages of upholstery and renovation.

He spun around when a woman called out from behind him. She popped her head out from behind an old wardrobe and said, 'Sorry, I'm here.'

Walking towards him, she wiped her hands on an oil cloth. 'Hi, I'm Eloise, what can I do for you?'

Simon had expected a man because the name above the barn said, 'Alan Thompson - Second Time Around.'

He told her this and she sighed. 'Yeah, my husband's name is still on there but I'm the one who does the upcycling work,' she said. 'Now that we've divorced, I'll need to change the sign, along with many other things.'

Eloise was small with a mass of ginger curly hair. She wore green dungarees and had a smudge of grease down her cheek.

He liked Eloise on sight and smiled at her. 'Oh, right,' he said. 'Well, I've been given an old cabinet and wondered if you could do something with it? I don't want to take it to the tip because I hate waste in any shape or form.'

She nodded. 'Me, too, and you thought of upcycling the cabinet?'

'Yeah, I watched the TV programme, 'Money For Nothing' and thought if I got it revamped then I could try and sell it and give the money to charity.'

Eloise grinned. 'That's a popular show and a good idea. Plus, I have a list of people who regularly buy from me so that might be another avenue.'

She looked around him and asked, 'So, where's the cabinet?'

Simon jerked his thumb over his shoulder. 'It's in the car – shall I fetch it?'

'That would help,' she said and laughed.

Simon hurried out to his car feeling more upbeat than he had for a couple of weeks. It hadn't been an easy time since New Year, and he opened the boot then hauled out the cabinet. Eloise was nice, he thought, and she filled him with confidence that something could be done to get rid of the cabinet. He carried it back into the barn and set it down on the floor.

She began to walk around examining it and opened two of the drawers at the front. Her small pixie-like face was animated at her task, and he could tell she was good at her job. Maybe she was looking for wood-worm, Simon thought remembering how they did this on the TV show.

She knelt down to look underneath the cabinet but hadn't spoken. Simon felt the need to fill the silence. 'So, let's call it an unwanted Christmas present,' he said and frowned. 'I'll never use it and the cabinet will always hold bitter-sweet memories for me.'

Eloise stopped her inspection and tilted her head to one side then looked up at him.

Simon stared into her small grey eyes which looked full of concern.

'Ah, I see,' she said. 'It's strange how little things can hold memories and creep up on us without warning, isn't it?'

Simon felt his shoulders slump. As opposed to the previous weeks when he hadn't wanted to talk with friends or family about the break-up of his marriage, now he felt the need to do so. Maybe it was because he knew Eloise had gone through the same and would know how it felt.

'My wife gave it to me on Christmas Day and I think she'd bought it in a second hand shop. She'd thought it perfect for my small garage where I tinker with things on my bike,' he said and shook his head. 'But what I found out on New Year's Eve rocked my world, or what I saw her doing with another man did.'

Eloise straightened up now and looked into his eyes. 'It's horrible catching them out,' she said and sighed. 'Alan was such an idiot that he didn't have the sense to cover his tracks!'

Simon tutted. 'Well, I saw my wife at our own New Year's Eve party in the kitchen kissing another man while I was in the lounge with guests,' he said. 'But she wasn't an idiot – she knew and always had done, exactly what she was doing.'

Eloise nodded and stroked the wood on the cabinet. 'Oh, I'm sorry to hear that – it must be all pretty raw for you?'

He grimaced. 'You could say that. My wife had a smile for every man who looked at her because she was beautiful, but I'd always thought it was me who had her heart,' he said. 'She had to be star of the show, but that was fine, because I'd been content to wait in the wings for her.'

She looked down at the floor and said, 'Well, Alan wasn't a particularly good-looking man, but he did have a certain something – a charisma, I'd thought when I first met him.'

Simon sighed imagining his wife. 'Well, taking selfies was her passion but I'd never minded because she took great pride in her appearance.'

Eloise wiped down the side of her face with the palm of her hand and tutted to herself when she saw the grease mark. He knew that she was thinking about her appearance and fought the urge to stretch over and gently remove the last traces of grease. Although it didn't matter to him. Simon knew she was confident and looked cute, but slightly vulnerable all at the same time.

Now he'd started to talk, he couldn't seem to stop. He said, 'It was impossible for her to pass by a mirror without glancing at herself with a self-satisfied smirk on her lips. At the time I'd accepted this as just the way she was, but now I can see it was pure conceit.'

Eloise had a faraway look in her eyes, and he knew she was thinking of Alan. 'We accept many things in marriage, Simon,' she said. 'I totally overlooked Alan's lies and deceit because I didn't want to face up to the fact that he wasn't the man I'd thought he was.'

Her eyes had clouded over now, and he felt bad that he'd dampened the earlier cheerful atmosphere. 'Sorry, I'm bringing back stuff from your marriage by rattling on about mine.'

The ginger curls shimmered when she shook her head. 'Nooo, it's fine – it's always good to talk.'

He cringed. 'And I can't bear to think how much of my hard-earned money she'd spent on clothes, shoes and handbags over the years,' he said. 'But I'd wanted to keeping her happy and content at home. And, of course, I'd loved her.'

He shook his head in disbelief that he was slagging his wife off like this with a stranger. Years ago, he would have defender her to the hilt but not now. The change in his thoughts and feelings towards her had altered and he knew this was for the best. There'd been enough mopping around since New Year, and now it was time to put it behind him and move on.

Eloise nodded. 'Well, all I can say is that it does get easier in time, and I learned to forgive myself because at the end of the day, I hadn't been in the wrong.'

8

Listening to her words, he knew they made sense. It cheered him to think there may be a light at the end of his dark tunnel. Simon could tell Eloise was a good listener by the way she let him talk and the gentle warm encouragement in her eyes.

Trying to lighten the tone, he said, 'And she must have been the first woman ever to wear a pink shell-suit with high heels!'

They laughed together and Eloise said, 'It sounds like we are both better off without them.'

He nodded. It had taken a while to get used to the change of feelings towards his wife. However, he was quickly getting used to Eloise's natural smile. It wasn't forced or painted on with lipstick for attention - it was genuinely meant.

Simon touched the top of the cabinet. 'So, have you had any ideas how to revamp it?'

She chuckled. 'Well, give me two weeks with the cabinet and around £150,' she said. 'And if I can transform it into something that looks completely different then you might want to keep it?'

This thought snaked its way through his mind, and he nodded. Eloise could well be right - if there was no resemblance to what it had been then maybe it might work.

Simon looked over and pointed at a pink dressing table. He grinned. 'Perhaps, but all I can say is when you come to upcycling, I'm not really a frilly-pink man!'

Eloise threw her head back and laughed. 'No, I can see that - I think you're more of a classic grey man.'

He smiled. 'You've got me in one.'

Shuffling his feet, he knew it was time to leave but hesitated. It suddenly struck him that he didn't want to leave her – he wanted to continue talking but not about his wife. He wanted to find out more about Eloise and get to know her better. She certainly had his interest piqued. He was impressed with her craftmanship and professionalism. Working all his life at accountancy in a Corbridge company her ideas and creative imagination fascinated him.

He shook his head knowing it was far too early to even think of meeting someone else. Over the last few weeks, he'd decided, it was a time to spend on his own.

He might never meet another woman but that hadn't worried or upset him. Aged forty, there was no rush to think that far ahead. Should he ask Eloise if he could take her out? But, how did he do that? He was so far out of touch with dating and how things worked that it was laughable. He rubbed his chin and started to walk slowly to the door.

Eloise joined him and touched the side of his arm. 'And when you come back, Simon, I'll have a pot of coffee on the go.'

His chest surged with happiness knowing she'd been on the same wavelength and hopefully was looking forward to him returning. Simon whistled leaving the barn knowing already that he was excited, not only to see what the cabinet would look like, but also to see Eloise again.

Valentine's Day Calamity

What part of, 'it's over' does this guy not understand? Alice puzzled over the valentine card. A friend had said, 'It's an anonymous poem so it might not be from him?'

But Alice knew his handwriting. Now, she was hurrying home to Birtley with a bag of groceries. Alighting from the bus at the top of Vigo estate, she noted that all the snow and ice had gone now and trundled down the pavement to her house. She took one step from the path onto the road to cross over, and that was it – down she went.

The thud on the corner of her glasses as they banged into the edge of her eyebrow seemed deafening. She hadn't seen the black ice in the gutter, but it felt cold on her cheek as she lay flat on her face.

'Oooh, Alice,' she heard an elderly woman cry.

Alice lifted her head to see the lady from the opposite bungalow calling for someone. A tall man rushed from her house. However, he didn't stop to help her at first, but hurried down the road after two wayward tins of baked beans that had escaped her carrier bag and were rolling in the gutter.

Sitting herself upright, Alice removed her mangled glasses and could smell blood. Having nursed for years in her younger days, she knew the smell all too well. Something was bleeding. Alice placed her hand to her cheek and felt the characteristic wet stickiness.

The man was behind her now tucking the beans back into her carrier bag and with his other strong arm he helped her up and onto her feet again.

'Are you okay?' He asked.

'I...I think so,' she said and mumbled her thanks.

Alice tried a few tentative steps and nodded. 'Yeah, nothing else seemed to have become detached from my body,' she said and tried to smile.

'Come on, let's get you home,' he said.

Alice looked at him and although her vision was blurred, she knew instantly he must be her neighbours son. The old woman had talked about him working abroad and Alice knew he couldn't have got this glowing healthy tan here in February.

He guided Alice across to her house as though she was blind which, considering her poor eyesight without the varifocal glasses, wasn't far off the mark. Thankfully, she'd a habit of taking out her keys on the bus and tucking them into her coat pocket which helped. Alice leaned against the porch window and produced the key ring so he could open her door.

Thanking him again, she stepped inside while he dropped the carrier bag onto the porch carpet.

'I don't think it's as bad as it looks,' he said. 'Things seldom are.'

Alice held out the slightly distorted glasses in her hand. 'Well, without these I can't see much unless it's up close,' she said and felt around the corner of the frame. 'I can tell these won't fit back on my face again.'

She staggered along the hallway and into the lounge and at her bidding, he followed her.

He asked, 'Have you a spare pair of glasses?'

Brilliant idea, she thought and smiled. Now why hadn't she thought of that? It was probably the shock she decided and plonked down onto the sofa with trembling legs.

She pointed to the bureau in the corner. 'My old ones might be in there?'

He hurried over and began to look through the mess inside the bureau. She sighed, but everyone had messy cupboards like this – didn't they? Note to oneself, tidy up the clutter.

'Got them!' He cried as though he'd found buried treasure. 'And now, a first aid kit?'

She shrugged then remembered a tin in the kitchen cupboard with Elastoplast's. Alice moved to the edge of the sofa to get up but didn't think her legs would carry her and slumped back again.

'Nooo, sit still,' he said.

She smiled. 'Along the passage and in the tall kitchen cupboard is an old M&S biscuit tin.'

Alice cringed, hoping she hadn't left the kitchen too messy this morning before leaving for work. However, she hadn't expected company, especially not a nice man. He set off in search of the tin and she eased her duffle coat back from her shoulders. She could hear the tap running and cupboard doors opening and closing. He returned carrying a bowl of warm water and the tin tucked under his arm.

From somewhere in her distant memory, Alice remembered his mam saying that he worked for an international health charity. Was he a doctor? Or a nurse? He certainly looked capable, she thought as he knelt down in front of her. He looked casual but attractive in blue jeans and a green fisherman sweater which she knew his mam had knitted for him.

'Let's see if we can clean off this blood and assess the damage,' he said. 'By the way, I'm Dan.'

Alice nodded and watched him open the tin. Dan lifted out a packet of gauze and tore along the top.

'And, I'm Alice,' she said.

Carefully he soaked a thick piece of gauze in the bowl of warm water and wiped down the side of her face and cheek. It felt bliss. Now he was close up to her she could see his big brown eyes and slight goatee beard. Hmm, she thought, Dan was nice and good to look at.

'Oh, I know who you are,' he said. 'Mam has told me all about you and how you've helped with her shopping when she was sheltered and, cut her grass last year.'

She smiled. 'Oh, that wasn't a problem, your mam's a lovely lady.'

And Dan has a very gentle touch, she thought. He was miles away from her ex-boyfriend who could be quite rough at times and wouldn't have a clue how to cope with this calamity.

Dan said, 'Now that's better, I can see where the blood has come from and it's only a small cut on the side of your eyebrow.'

'Oh that's good - are there any sticky plasters in that tin?'

Carefully, she put her old glasses back on and could see him properly. Concern showed in his face, and he sat back on his hunkers. Dan shook his head. 'Now, I'm not an expert, but I think this needs a little more than a plaster – maybe steri-strips to knit it together?'

Alice laid her head back on the sofa and took a deep sigh of resignation. 'So, that's a trip to the QE hospital,' she said. 'I'll ring my sister.'

Dan stood up. 'Well, if she's not available - I can take you?'

She looked at him and smiled. 'Thanks, but I think I've taken up enough time from the visit with your mam.'

He shook his head. 'Nooo, it's not a visit - I'm staying with her until I start my new job and find somewhere to live,' he said and grinned. 'And although she would never say, I think she's sick of me under her feet all day!'

As Alice dialled her sister's number, she sighed. 'Ah, no, I've remembered she's out for the day with her friends.'

'That's it then,' Dan said. 'I'll go and get my car.'

She smiled her thanks. When Dan returned and stood in the porch, he eased her carrier bag aside with his foot. She groaned when the Valentine card slid out onto the carpet.

They both looked down at the card.

'Aww, I'd forgotten it's the 14^{th of} February. So, who's a lucky girl, or is it from a secret admirer?'

Alice grimaced following him out to the car. 'Not me because I know who it's from.'

Dan opened the car door for her while she said, 'It was over last year but maybe he thought of this as a last ditch effort.'

'Well,' Dan said driving up the road. 'I can't blame the guy for trying – I wouldn't give up without a fight either.'

She'd felt her insides tumble and knew it wasn't the shock of falling. She liked Dan. And could tell, or hoped the feeling was mutual. They chatted easily waiting in A&E at The Queen Elizabeth Hospital, and Alice decided it was good to have him with her.

While the nurse treated her eyebrow, she pondered over his comment about the Valentine card. She remembered his mam saying, 'I wish Dan would settle down and give me some grandchildren.'

Did this mean he was on his own too? With a dressing over her eyebrow, she returned to Dan in the waiting room.

'The nurse doesn't think it'll leave a scar,' she said and smiled.

'Now that's great,' he said. 'I'm glad there's not much damage to that pretty face of yours.'

She felt her cheeks flush and knew he was flirting with her. 'Ah, flattery will get you everywhere,' she laughed.

His eyes filled with concern. 'Nooo, Alice, I wasn't teasing,' he said and shuffled his feet on the floor. 'I meant it.'

They walked out of A&E, and she felt his hand on the small of her back as they negotiated their way through the swing doors. It felt nice. It made her feel secure as though she was in safe hands. Unlike her ex who wouldn't have even come to the hospital with her.

Alice felt at ease in Dan's company, so much so that she didn't want to leave him when they pulled onto their street. As he parked the car outside her house, she looked further down the path and hooted.

'Oh look, there's my cabbage in the hedge - it must have rolled out from the carrier bag when I fell?'

They both laughed as she hurried to pick it up. Alice wanted to see him again but felt out of practise with men and didn't know what to say. He was beside her in seconds and they stood looking at each other with the cabbage between them.

'So, what are you going to do with that?' Dan asked, 'Mam told me you were a good cook and often took her homemade scones.'

Alice smiled. 'Well, I was going to make belly pork and creamed cabbage with butter and black pepper.'

Dan licked his big lips. 'I don't suppose there'd be enough for two?'

Laughing, she said, 'Of course there will – about seven?'

Dan returned across the street and did a little jump kicking his heels which made her giggle.

At seven, Alice heard him knock on the porch door. She opened the door, and he promptly handed her a bunch of red roses and a card. She grinned at him.

'Well, as it's Valentine's Day, and after the awful day you've had, I thought you deserved another card,' he said and stared into her eyes.

She read the card and cocked her head to one side. 'Well, my day hasn't been all that bad because I met you!'

The Food Bank

Angela watches her husband, Michael heading out of the door and sighs. He has called goodbye in his usual manner but as she rinses her cup in the sink the hairs on the back of her neck stand up.

Michael is an ex-firefighter who had to leave his job after a knee operation. She knows how attractive, engaging, and sociable he is to everyone, especially women. Angela frowns thinking of how other women look at him with longing and their jokes about being rescued from a burning building over his shoulder.

Watching him walk through the garden gate Angela realises it is the third time this week that he has left the house at the same time. Ordinarily when she's at work his comings and goings aren't known to her but with being on holiday, she has noticed his daily routine.

He had called out, 'Just going for a walk.'

Angela had offered to join him, but he'd replied, 'No, thanks, I like to walk on my own.'

Now, she thinks of his words, on my own and a shiver runs up her back. He wouldn't cheat on her, would he? Angela grabs her jacket and decides to follow him.

Walking behind him at a distance, she knows his gait and slight limp so well. In fact, she knows everything about him after ten years of happy marriage. And, it has been happy, she thinks, but lately, well maybe he hasn't looked so content. It had been a big adjustment leaving the job he loved and even though he'd been offered a job working in the office of a car sales room in Benwell, Michael had refused.

She bites her lip knowing that if he sees her following and doubting him, he will be dreadfully hurt. Angela can tell he is heading for Newcastle town centre now and she kicks a pebble on the path with her boot. This is crazy, she thinks but all the same the need to know where he is going pushes her onwards. He reaches Benwell Lane but turns down towards a pale green prefab building.

Perspiration forms on her top lip and she takes a deep breath. Where is he going? Is he meeting another woman in there? Surely not, she sighs and looks around at the area. If he were having a clandestine affair, it wouldn't be here, would it? It would be in a hotel or a bedroom in someone's house? The thought of him in another woman's bedroom makes her stomach roll and she stifles a small cry.

Angela slows her pace and hangs back a little. She racks her brain to think if there have been any tell-tale signs of a secret affair but shakes her head. No cliché lipstick on his collar, nor smell of a different perfume to hers. But there again, she sighs, up until now she's had no cause to rifle through his pockets looking for hotel or restaurant receipts.

It's windy and cold and she shudders but not from the weather. It is more from the fear that is clutching at her chest. If he is seeing someone else and she is about to lose him the

devastation didn't bear thinking about.
Noooo, her mind screams, please don't let it
be another woman. She'd loved and idolised
him from the very first night they'd met at a
party. Michael had easily been the best-
looking guy in the room and by the end of
New Year's Eve, she had known he was the
one. The one she would spend the rest of her
life with.

Angela hides behind an old stone wall
watching him open the big door to the
prefab. There is a wood billboard near the
door, and she curses under her breath.
Without her glasses she can't read from a
distance.

Furtively, she nears the door while he goes
inside. She creeps further to the board and
gasps aloud. The sign reads, 'Newcastle
Food Bank – West End.'

Angela takes a deep breath and tugs open
the door then peeks inside. It's a big room
with grubby strip lighting on the ceiling.
Grey shelves line the walls and in the middle
are long countertops. She steps inside and
looks around. She's never been inside a food
bank before and stares at the shelves stocked
with tins, packets, and boxes of food. It's a
little like a supermarket, she thinks, except
there are no price tags of course.

Laughter is coming from behind the long
shelving at the back of the room and she
recognises Michael's low throaty laugh. She
hurries forward just as he appears carrying a
big cardboard box with two older ladies
tottering along behind him.

Michael stops dead in his tracks when he sees her. 'Angela! What are you doing here?'

She folds her arms across her chest and huffs loudly. 'More to the point, Michael, what are you doing here?'

The nearest lady to Angela steps towards her. She is wearing a black and white knitted hat. 'Ah, so you're, Angela,' she says. 'Michael has told us all about you and we'd hoped you'd come along one day to meet us. I'm Doris and this is Jean.'

Angela clicks her tongue and glares at her husband. 'Well, I would have done if I'd been invited!'

Remembering her previous doubts, Angela looks behind him to see if there is anybody else around. She sees him follow her gaze over his shoulder.

He raises an eyebrow and frowns, 'What?'

Feeling foolish because there are no other women in sight, Angela sighs heavily and deflates like a balloon. The pent-up anxiety that has flooded through her since she left home dissolves and she licks her dry lips.

The door behind them opens and another two men enter the room cheering. One of them calls out, 'Hey, Michael, how's it going?'

The other man looks at his watch and shouts, 'Not long now until opening, and we've got some great fresh fruit today!'

Doris and Jean sidle past Angela and join the men while they open bags packed with satsumas and peaches. Ooh, and aah noises are made while they help to unpack and assemble the fruit.

Angela steps forwards to Michael and asks quietly, 'So, are you working here?'

Michael nods and places the box on the floor. He shoves his hands inside his jean pockets.

She stares at him. 'But why didn't you tell me?'

He shrugs his shoulders. 'Because you'd make a fuss and tell me I should be resting my knee.'

She stares into his eyes knowing this is true. 'Well, yes, but only because I'm concerned, and the doctor told you not to return to a manual heavy job.'

He smiles. 'Em, the doctor told me not to go back to fire-fighting, but he did say that I'd soon gauge my own limitations which I have now. And I can manage working here with no problems.'

She looks around the room and wrinkles her nose. 'B…but you didn't want the office job when it was offered, so I can't understand, why here?'

Michael sighs and shuffles his trainers on the squeaky lino floor. 'Because I'm used to helping people, Angela, and I miss the community spirit. It's what I've always done, and I know how to do this,' he said frowning. 'I don't know how to sit in an office!'

Angela hears the men open the doors declaring the food bank open. Michael takes her arm and eases her to the side of the shelving as an old man and woman enter carrying a wicker shopping basket. Two younger women with three small children follow them and they all step up to the counter in the middle of the room. An Indian man with a teenager stands in line behind the children.

Angela watches the people in the queue and sighs. She decides there is an air of shame hanging around their bent heads while they stand quietly looking at the small crates of groceries. It's almost as if they are embarrassed to accept the food on offer. A steady stream of all ages, genders, and ethnicity enter the room and she sighs.

Angela chews the inside of her cheek. She feels terrible for her misgivings about Michael. Why had she thought he was cheating on her? He'd never given her cause for concern before. She looks at his big strong arms lifting the crates then smiles. His knee may well be damaged now but he's still big and sturdy. And he is such a good man. Angela shakes her head; how could she have forgotten that?

Doris and Jean simper at him while he teases them.

Michael is right, he doesn't belong in an office working alone at a desk. This is where he belongs amongst people. People who he can help with a sense of civic pride.

The more people that enter the food bank, the more flustered Doris and Jean become. Angela can see they are struggling to keep up with people's requests and without hesitation she strips off her jacket. She lays it aside and steps up next to Doris. Angela helps them place fruit inside the crates and works at a much faster pace.

'Hey, thanks, you're good at this,' Jean says. 'Much quicker than us.'

Angela grins. 'Well, if I'd known Michael was coming here, I would have joined him sooner.'

There's an air of team spirit in the room from the small band of helpers and it makes Angela feel good.

She sees Michael grinning at her when he slides crate after crate along the counter.

'Hey, it's great for us to be working together at last,' he shouts.

She smiles and nods back. It did feel good to be helping with such a worthwhile cause. But what felt even better was seeing the look on a small child's face as he bit into a peach and licked the juice from his chin.

Angela swallows a lump in her throat knowing he has probably never tasted a fresh peach before.

When most of the crates have been taken, she feels Michael behind her wrapping his arms around her waist and nuzzling into her neck.

'Oh, Michael,' she whispers. 'These poor people have nothing.'

He nods and she can feel his warm breath on her ear. 'I know, that's why I want to help and give something back to the community.'

'Well, if it's open on a weekend,' she says hugging him close. 'I can come to help Doris and Jean?'

He squeezes her tight. 'That'll be great,' he says. 'And I know these people have got nothing but that makes me feel even luckier because I've got you!'

Leap Year

Thanks to Julius Caesar we have an extra day every four years, Emma thought staring into the mirror. The last was in 2020 and she would have to wait another two years for the next one, but she didn't want to – she wanted to get engaged now.

It was a day when a woman could propose to a man thanks to a tradition began by Irish monks who took this to Scotland in 1288. The monks stipulated that a woman must wear a red petticoat when proposing and the man would be fined if he refused. Rifling through her wardrobe, she realised that she didn't possess such a thing, but she did have red underwear – would this do?

Mark loved her, didn't he? He told her often enough, but she bit her lip. He'd already paid a parking fine this month and she giggled not wanting to see him fined twice.

Emma had been born on 29th February and knew that as a leapling she could celebrate her birthday on 28th February or the 1st of March. Her mam had declared on her first birthday that it would be in February which was today, and Mark was taking her out to Blackfriars Restaurant in Newcastle for dinner.

Last year they'd been at a friend's wedding at Blackfriars. The location was central, and the olde-worlde medieval setting was amazing. The food was good at what Mark thought as a reasonable rate. Emma had hoped the ceremony would spur him into action, but it hadn't.

However, Mark had given her a small present on Christmas Day and when she'd torn off the wrapping paper and bow, Emma had gasped. The little box had been black with a jewellers mark and her heart had soared in hope. The vision of him down on one knee proclaiming his love and proposing had been dashed when she'd flipped up the lid and saw the gold ear rings. Although they were lovely her heart had sunk – it hadn't been the engagement ring she'd dreamt about.

Now, wearing her red underwear and little black dress, she looked across the table in the restaurant at Mark and smiled. Instead of waiting for him to make the move, Emma determined that she was going to propose to him, leap year or not.

They'd had a lovely meal and two glasses of a good red wine. Her stomach felt too full of butterflies to eat dessert, but he had taken an age picking at cheese and crackers. However, she smiled, that was Mark with endless patience who took life slowly, and carefully considered each decision he made. Her mam often said, 'Which is the total opposite to you, Emma who rushes in life at a hundred miles an hour!'

Emma took a deep breath and relaxed her shoulders. She decided to take a leaf out of his book and gradually work the conversation around to their future together before she proposed. Emma wanted to remember every tiny detail about this special moment between them. She, of course, wouldn't get down on one knee because of the old wood flooring, and her dress was too short. Nor did she have a ring to give him as she hadn't been paid yet.

Emma smiled, but she did have her proposal speech ready and knew exactly how she would declare her love for him. She'd tell him how she wanted to be with him for the rest of her life. How she could never look at another man and that his kind gentle personality had won her over completely.

Mark seemed to be agitated now and Emma wondered if his indigestion was kicking-in after the meal. She watched him shuffle on the seat and heard the rubber soles of his shoes squeaking on the tiled floor.

'Emma,' he said and fiddled with the cutlery on the table.

After two years of living together she knew his every move and could tell what was going through his mind before he even thought about it himself. He had that serious, worried look on his face with his bushy eyebrows drawn together.

She knew this was something big, but what was he going to say? A chill of doubt curled around her stomach, and she swallowed hard. Was he going to finish with her? Emma couldn't bear it if he did and wondered if she should jump in first with her proposal. She didn't know what to do and bit her lip whilst looking around people at nearby tables as if they would have the answer to her predicament.

Suddenly, Mark pushed away from the table and dropped to his knee. She almost cried out aloud in surprise and felt her insides tumble in pure happiness. Emma eyed the bulge in his trouser pocket as he pulled out a small red box and popped open the lid. 'I've loved you since the day we met, Emma and I want you to be my wife,' he said. 'Will you marry me?'

Working From Home

Lauren sat on the end of the sofa crunching muesli while her mam was in the shower. She yawned. Mam had been up twice during the night in a confused state. Lauren hated what this awful Alzheimer's disease was doing to her lovely mam.

Lauren glanced at a news interview on TV where the local Morpeth councillor was talking from his home office. There was something vaguely familiar about his face.

The viewers could see around his office area and over the last two years Lauren had got used to looking at everyone's backgrounds. She smiled, it was like the kitchen adverts which said, 'Cure your house embarrassment now!'

Staring at the TV screen she saw a small plant on a stand in the corner of his office and a large bookshelf behind him which obviously held much-loved favourite books. Lauren wasn't really listening to what he was saying about Morpeth and the Wansbeck river, but stared closer at the background to his desk. On the end of the shelf were three photographs. One, obviously of older grandparents, another with him and a group of friends wearing rugby shirts and the last photograph was in a shiny chrome frame.

The camera zoomed in closer to him and Lauren dropped her bowl of muesli with a clatter onto the coffee table. She cried out, 'That's me! I'm in that photograph with him!'

Lauren grabbed the remote and quickly pressed record to save the interview so that she could look at it again. She had to make sure it was her and wasn't imaging things like her mam. Lauren shook her head abruptly and dropped to her knees in front of the TV screen to get a better view.

'It's Liam,' she gasped under her breath. Sporting a full beard and wearing glasses he had changed so much that she would have walked past him in the street. Unless, of course, she was up close to him because she would never mistake those dark green eyes. Lauren shivered; she'd always felt they could see right through her.

The interview finished and Lauren pressed play back. She zoomed in closer and stared at the photograph. It had been taken way back in 2005 when they were on the dodgems at The Hopping's on the town moor. He was laughing with his head thrown back because she had dunched into him, and she was giggling too. Gosh, we looked so young back then, she mused, and remembered The Hopping's like it was yesterday.

Memories tumbled back through the five months they had spent together and how at eighteen, she'd thought they were so much in love. Liam had been her first and she remembered how they'd made out in the back of his car. Lauren grinned. He'd been a good man. Decent, honest, and caring, in fact, he'd been everything her ex-husband hadn't been.

Liam loved their town, Morpeth and she wasn't surprised he'd become a councillor. He had chosen to study at Newcastle University after secretly admitting he wouldn't have the courage to go down south.

Whereas, she had gone off to Nottingham to study forensics. 'Of course, we'll stay together - long distances can work,' she'd said. But, it hadn't and that was seventeen years ago.

Helping her mam dress for the day, she wondered why he had kept the photograph? Lauren scoured the old bedroom and found her photo album then sighed. she'd thrown her copy away, in fact, she'd ditched all her past to please her husband.

However, she thought, it would be easy enough to get in touch with Liam. But did she really want to? She shrugged, he was probably married with a family, but if so, why would he have a photograph of her on his bookshelf? She swallowed hard. No wife would want a photograph of an old flame on their bookshelves, would they? She knew she wouldn't.

For the third time that morning, Lauren stressed to her mam, 'But we can't go down the coast - it's far too cold and snow is forecast.'

With so many questions but no answers, she Googled Liam and jotted down his contact details. She discovered that he'd been a widower for two years, and strangely, he hadn't had any children either. Should she ring or email him?

Lauren sighed. After moving back to Morpeth to care for her mam the days were full-on, and she had little free time to herself. And, she frowned, who knew whether Mam had a long or short journey ahead, or exactly what this would entail. However, having the support of an old friend along the way might just help?

While her mam dozed in the chair, Lauren held her mobile in a trembling hand and tapped in his number then took a deep breath….

Mother's Day in Blyth

Joyce knew that Ellen at number seven would have been inundated with Mother's Day cards again because she always was. Ellen was a mother three times over. Whereas her own windowsill was empty. Yet another Mothering Sunday with nothing from her daughter. She spied out of her curtain across at number seven watching Ellen's car pull off the drive.

Tugging on her jacket against a stiff March wind, she hurried across and down the side path to Ellen's back garden. Joyce knew snooping around her neighbours wasn't a nice thing to do and if she really wanted to see how many cards Ellen had received all she had to do was invite herself inside for a coffee. They'd been friends for years now living close to the seafront in Blyth. But she found it embarrassing to admit that she hadn't received anything, yet again.

Joyce approached the lounge window and furtively looked over her shoulder. No one was in sight and their back gardens were not overlooked. Suddenly, she heard a man's voice shout, and she jumped back narrowly missing the cat who sped off across the lawn. Joyce groaned as she heard the planter smash into pieces behind her. Cursing under her breath, she quickly scurried back across to number four.

When Ellen returned from shopping, she could tell by the smashed terracotta planter that someone has been in her beloved garden. She looked at the footage on her security camera and saw Joyce creeping around then staring into the lounge window. Her son had bought the camera as a Christmas present and Ellen zoomed in closer on the screen. Joyce's face looked twisted with resentment, and she sighed, but why? She imagined Joyce mumbling through clenched teeth about her cards, flowers and chocolates.

Ellen made lunch and decided to arrange a coffee morning for her two neighbours. It wasn't the first time she'd seen Joyce snooping around and knew she couldn't ignore it any longer. Something had to be done.

Christine, from number nine arrived early the next morning and Ellen explained what had happened. She liked Christine who was a quiet, shy lady that only seemed to come to life when her husband returned from working off shore.

Christine wrung her hands. 'Oh, Ellen, I don't like confrontation it upsets my stomach.'

Ellen reassured her. 'It's okay, you don't have to say a word and needn't get involved at all, but it'll be good to have a witness.'

Joyce arrived in a flurry complaining about her daughter who'd turned up late asking to borrow money again. She groaned. 'Not a Mother's Day card in sight,' she said. 'Neither her nor her useless husband are working now, and she's taken to visiting the food bank in Blyth shopping centre!'

Christine sighed. 'Oh, that must be such a worry for you, Joyce.'

Joyce nodded and sipped her coffee. 'Of course, but I give in to her because of the grandchildren – I can't bear to think they're doing without.'

Ellen nodded and looked at Joyce's face. It was what some people would call sour until she smiled and then her whole face lit up. She took a deep breath and told Joyce what she'd seen on the security camera. 'This has to stop, Joyce,' she said. 'And I won't take it any further this time, but I would like to know why?'

Joyce looked across at Ellen's cards and pouted. 'Because you always get so much given, and I get nothing!'

Sighing, Ellen said, 'Yes, but my kids live miles away in Scotland and Liverpool. I never get to see them that's why they send cards and flowers. I'd rather have them call in regularly for a chat like your daughter does. I'd give up the cards tomorrow if I could only see them at my doorstep on Mother's Day.'

Christine nodded in agreement. 'Yeah, and my son only lives in Seaton Sluice but because of the woman he married I never get to see him,' she said. 'My daughter-in-law won't even know that he's chosen and sent me a card – she'd be furious.'

Ellen said, 'So, Joyce, you can see we all have different families but as far as I can tell you're the lucky one to have your daughter close to you.'

Tears slid down Joyce's face and she nodded. 'I...I know, you're right but it makes me feel like a lousy Mother,' she said. 'And I'm sorry about the planter, Ellen I will replace it.'

Ellen melted and waved her hand in dismissal. She reached over and gave her a big hug. 'But you're a great Mother! And next year, me and Christine will buy you a card to put on your windowsill just so you don't feel left out.'

Joyce wiped her tears away and gave them a weak smile of thanks.

Cottage on the Hill

Stephen drove as quickly as possible through the water-logged roads to Otley in Yorkshire. He was desperate to see his mum after the storm. She still lived in their old family home up on the hill above the town. It was a white stone cottage which stood out in the landscape surrounded by a forest of trees.

He grimaced remembering the sentence she often said in his response to moving, 'You'll take me out of here in my coffin!'

It wasn't a big cottage just two small bedrooms, but it was where he and his sister had been raised. Mum had lived there sixty-one years and there was no shifting her. His father had died years ago and now his mum was eighty and alone. It was a constant worry to him and his wife, Beth who adored his mum too. Over the last few years, he'd pleaded and begged for her to sell up, but she flatly refused.

Storm Eunice had raged the day before and although he'd tried twice to drive from Ilkley to Otley the road had been flooded then impassable by a fallen tree. When he'd previously looked at the weather forecast, they'd wanted her to come and stay with them. But she'd adamantly shaken her head and reassured him she would be fine.

Stephen chewed the bottom of his moustache and turned right into the town. He redialled her number again from the hands-free but still there was no answer. He groaned and rubbed his eye which felt full of grit because he'd hardly slept.

The noise of the storm outside their bedroom window had been bad enough but the worry of his mum alone in the cottage had kept him awake tossing and turning. He'd gazed out of their bedroom window at the ravaged countryside with streaks of silver lightening speeding across the darkness of the sky and shuddered.

Did she have power? Had she found the candles? Was she shivering with cold in her bedroom? Had she fallen on the stairs in the dark? Or worse still, fallen carrying a candle and the cottage had burned down around her? Had any of the old trees outside come down and crashed through the windows?

His mind had spun with fear because he couldn't reach her. There'd been no answer on either her mobile or landline. Part of him had raged against what he saw as her stubbornness to live there in her old age and thought it selfish.

He knew and understood the memories of their family home but all the same, he fretted every day about her. Not that he wanted her to go into an old people's home because he didn't, but last year he'd spotted a small bungalow in town for sale and had taken her the details. In her usual obstinate manner, she'd tutted and refused to even look at them then tossed them onto the fire.

Stephen turned onto the narrow winding road uphill which was more of a rough dirt track than a proper road. He slowed down to a minimum because he could feel the earth was soft and wet under the car and didn't want to get stuck.

Beth had put fresh milk and bread with a few other necessities into the boot of his car this morning before he'd set off. She had wanted to join him, but he'd refused because he didn't know what awaited him at the cottage which might alarm her.

When Beth had given him the bag, she'd said, 'Stephen, it's her life and if Mum wants to stay up there alone that's up to her. You can't force her to leave. These are her decisions to make but do tell her again that we want her with us. I've got the guest bedroom ready just in case.'

Stephen smiled thinking of Beth. She was missing the two boys who had gone off to university and knew Beth was looking for someone to fuss over. It's what she did best.

He sighed however, and knew Beth was right about Mum making her own decisions but that didn't make it any easier for him.

He turned up the steeper hillside now and breathed a small sigh of relief. The track looked clear and because he knew all the trees and landscape as though he was blindfolded, he was confident there were no fallen trees.

He'd watched the storm news on TV early that morning with last night's images of trees crashing onto cars and into windows resulting in fatalities which had only fuelled his anxiety.

Stephen took a deep breath and tried to apply the logical side to his mind. In the past when he'd worried about her then arrived to see her waiting at the door and all was well, he'd chastised himself for fretting. But that wasn't following a storm, he thought. He could only hope and pray today would be the same.

However, as he neared the cottage she wasn't at the door. He chewed his moustache again and felt his stomach churn. Where was she? She had always been able to hear a car on the dirt track from any room in the house, so why not today?

Stephen turned off the ignition, took a deep breath to bolster himself for what lay ahead then hurried through the back door into the large kitchen. It was empty. His heart raced when he hurried through the lounge which was also empty. Then tearing to the bottom of the staircase to run up, his mouth dried, and he croaked, 'Mum? Where are you!'

Silence surrounded him and he choked back a sob in his throat. Dear God, where was she? Outside amongst the trees? On the bathroom floor?

But then his shoulders sank, and he felt near collapse when she tottered through the passage from the downstairs toilet.

'Oh, Mum!' He shouted and ran to her.

He wrapped her into his arms and sighed with relief. The fear left his body and his legs felt weak and shaky. He dropped down into his father's armchair by the side of the fireplace. He bent forward and put his head in his hands. 'I was so frightened that I'd find you had fallen down or worse?'

He felt her hand patting the top of his head then running her fingers through his hair. It reminded him of when he was little and had the same recurrent bad dream that he'd been lost amongst the trees and couldn't find his way home.

Stephen leaned into her and expected to find her soft ample waist where he'd often buried his head. Instead, he felt her thin craggy hip bones which brought him back to the here and now. He shook his head abruptly.

'I'll make some tea,' she said busying off into the kitchen. She called through to him, 'And thank Beth for the milk, she's so thoughtful because I had run out last night.'

Settled and sipping their hot tea, Stephen pulled a face. 'Urgh, there's sugar in this!'

'It's good for shock,' she muttered and handed him the biscuit barrel which was full of his favourite jammy dodgers and chocolate digestives. He grinned.

She said, 'Well, it was a horrible storm. Probably the worst I can remember up here unless my memory is playing tricks with me.'

Stephen licked the chocolate from his fingers and let her talk.

She looked past him and out of the window. 'The sky was black at just four in the afternoon as if it was the middle of the night. Then the TV crackled, and the screen was all white blotches, but it didn't go off.'

He nodded and sipped the hot tea.

'Then through the night the lightening cracked off the bedroom window,' she said. 'I suppose if the windows had been double glazed, I wouldn't have heard the claps of thunder which were deafening! And I did try to ring you, but the landline was off and of course there's very little mobile signal even on a good day.'

He saw her hand tremble when she lifted the teapot to pour more tea. Her eyes darted around the fireplace. 'Then yesterday, I thought there was something lodged in the old chimney,' she said. 'Because the noise was so scary…' she shivered and pulled a fluffy cardigan around her shoulders.

Stephen had installed a log burner last year and always made sure she had a stack of chopped logs but now he noticed she'd only used the smaller ones. Maybe the others were too heavy to lift? He picked up a big log and chucked it into the burner.

He saw her nod in satisfaction and his heart squeezed. He couldn't remember his mum ever using the word scary before, let alone look scared.

She looked old and shrivelled up somehow. Gone was her strong robust figure that she'd always had. He stared at her thin wasted arms which had been strong and chubby. A memory flashed through his mind of baking day when he was little. With flushed red cheeks and her sleeves rolled up to her elbows she'd roll out pastry to make pies and pasties. And how those big arms could hold him in a cuddle that near took his breath away.

But now she was small and frail. He gulped hard. If his father were here, he would be saddened to see her infirmity, and like himself, would think she was suffering in the cottage alone. But what else could he do?

'Yes, it was a bad night,' she said.

He sighed. 'Well, there's more to come according to the forecast because of this global warming,' he said. 'We can expect more flooding in the rivers as the rain moves down the hills and moors today.'

He saw her eyes widen at the thought. 'Well, at least I'm not near a river.'

He nodded and dunked another biscuit into his tea. 'No, but it means I can't get up to you every day if the roads on flooded!'

She nodded and stared into the burner.

He tried again. 'Please come and stay with us at least until the storm threats ease off then I'll get a good night's sleep not worrying about you up here alone?'

She nodded and he sensed an air of defeat around her wrinkled face.

He watched her take in a deep breath, then she said, 'Okay, I'll come until the weekend and maybe when I'm there, you could look for a small flat or bungalow near you?'

He gasped and quickly nodded in agreement before she could change her mind.

She smiled at him. 'I think it's time to say goodbye to the old place.'

Gramps in Birtley Garden Centre

'Mam is going to be so mad with us!'

Becky glared at her ten year old brother Tim. 'Well, it's all your fault – you were supposed to be staying with him!'

'It's not,' he wailed and kicked at the pebbled path. 'Gramps had two leeks in his hand the last time I saw him. I thought he was going to pay for them.'

Her younger brother, Joe, clung to her leg. She could feel his little body trembling and knew he was scared. He never liked family shouting. She put her arm around his shoulder and squeezed him tight. 'It's okay, don't worry,' she soothed.

Joe looked up at her with watery eyes. 'Maybe gramps is playing hide and seek?'

Becky shook her head. 'I don't think so, but we'll have to find him before Mam comes back from the toilets.'

Aged twelve, Becky sighed. Sometimes it wasn't much fun being the eldest. She knew her mam relied upon her to watch over the boys, but they were hard work, especially Tim who was never where he was supposed to be.

She made a quick decision. 'Right, we'll go off and find him before mam gets back then she'll never know any different.'

Tim pulled up his rolled-down sock and nodded.

'We'll split up and go two different ways around the rows of plants,' she said and felt Joe tug at the hem of her dress.

'Can I stay with you Becky?' Joe said. 'I...I don't want to go with Tim!'

She took his hand. Joe knew his older brother was always in trouble and that he'd be safer with her. Becky pulled back her shoulders.

Tim shouted, 'I'll go back this way to the vegetable seeds, and you go the other way.'

Becky said, 'Okay, but let's think about this logically.' She wasn't entirely sure if this was the right word to use but knew it would be what her mam would say. 'So, what is gramps wearing?'

Tim sighed and shrugged. 'Durr, we all know what he looks like – he's just gramps.'

Joe cried, 'He's got his brown anorak on and his black boots with the shiny toecaps because he told me it would be muddy.'

Becky clapped her hands. 'You see, Tim, our Joe is cleverer than you already and he's only seven.'

Tim pushed his hands deep into his pockets and strode off.

Becky shouted. 'Stay on the path, Tim and go around in the big circle then we'll meet back up here in ten minutes.'

Taking Joe by his hand, she set off in the opposite direction. 'Now, you keep looking at everyone's feet to see if you can spot his boots and I'll look out for his anorak.'

Birtley garden centre was busy, and they weaved their way in and out of people carrying baskets and pushing trolleys with trays of what gramps called, bedding plants.

She'd always giggled at this phrase because it sounded as though you were tucking-up plants at bedtime. Gramps had chuckled when she'd told him and said, 'You're not far wrong, Becky because the pansies need to be well looked after – I often read them a story at night.'

Becky bit her lip. Oh, where was he, she thought scanning the older people they passed. She loved gramps. They all did, and she couldn't bear anything awful happening to him. Gramps had a huge garden which Dad called an allotment, and they loved visiting him there. He usually had corned beef sandwiches and a big flask of tea which they'd have sitting on upturned plant pots. But lately, he hadn't been his usual self.

Mam told us that gramps was getting a bit confused as he got older and had used a word that she'd forgotten. It began with an A and had a Z in it which was tricky to spell.

They wandered past very tall plants and bushes which had a label saying, creepers. If she hadn't been worried, she would have thought this a funny name. But she couldn't laugh yet, not until they found gramps and knew he was safe.

They'd reached the big area at the back which held summerhouses and garden sheds.

Suddenly, Joe shouted, 'There he is! There are his boots!'

Becky spun around to see where Joe was pointing, and they hurried over to the smallest shed. In the open doorway was a blue stripped deckchair and gramps was sitting asleep with the two leeks on his knees.

She breathed a big sigh of relief and hurried over to him just as she heard Tim running around the gravel path.

'We've found him!' Becky yelled, then smiled to see her mam close behind Tim.

The Talisman

Captain Jones from The Durham Light Infantry was heading off to France once more. He was regarded by the troops as the boss and knew his main task was to inspire his men ready for battle. He needed to bolster them with confidence so that they could win this war and beat the Germans back from the shores of their beloved England. The captain looked smart in his uniform and pulled back his shoulders in pride – he was representing the army and his King.

He was a quiet man at home in the Durham miners cottage, but when organising the battle he was known by his troop as their talisman. A big man in heart and spirit – he always seemed to know what to do. He'd worn a leather chain around his neck in the last battle but it had been torn from him during the fighting.

His dad had given it to him and told him it would guard against evil and bring him good luck. 'I always wear one when I'm down the pit,' he'd said.

Unfortunately, it hadn't and Captain Jones had been slightly wounded. However, when he'd opened his eyes and seen the nurse looking over him he'd changed his mind and knew the leather chain had indeed brought him good luck. In his concussed state, he'd thought she looked like a blonde angel sent from heaven. He'd fallen for her when she tended his wound so gently and she'd quickly become his sweetheart.

But now it was time to return to the battlefield and his heart was heavy. He didn't want to leave her. Standing together in Durham train station on platform one, she twined her arms around his neck and he drew her into him.

After their last long lingering kiss, she gave him a rabbit's foot on a small keyring. 'It was given to me by my nana,' she said. 'And, it has kept me safe all my life.'

'Nooo, you keep it,' he said. 'I need you to stay safe until I come home – I want you to be here waiting for me!'

She'd smiled in what he'd thought was agreement but when he boarded the train and the sight of her disappeared from the platform, he'd felt something bulky in his trouser pocket.

Captain Jones pushed his hand inside and pulled out her rabbit's foot. He grinned knowing her talisman would definitely keep him safe this time.

Afternoon Tea

'But I'm hungry now,' wailed the Duchess of Northumberland. 'It's been hours since luncheon at one, and I simply cannot wait until eight for dinner!'

Her long-suffering maid, Alice, took a deep breath and soothed. 'Your friends will be here soon and we'll serve tea with the food,' she said. 'And they're not late – it is only ten minutes to four.'

The duchess complained, 'Ah, you'd think they could be early for once when I'm peckish and need something to fill the gap,' she said then shouted. 'Look, bring out the selection of sweet and savoury snacks now so I can nibble at something!'

Alice bobbed in front of her and scurried out of the sitting room. She skirted along the passage and down the spiral staircase of Alnwick Castle. 'Hmmph! Low tea, indeed,' she muttered pulling the lace-cap down over her forehead.

She flew into the kitchen area and caught up with the butler and cook who were standing chatting. She gasped, 'The duchess wants all the food taking upstairs now – she's hungry and doesn't intend to wait until her guests arrive.'

The butler jumped to attention. He snapped his fingers at the footmen who immediately rushed across the kitchen and picked up the silver platters.

The old cook grumbled and clicked her tongue. 'As if I haven't got enough work to do with three meals a day, now it's blooming four. It was bad enough having to make her ladyship a tray in her room with afternoon treats but now it's guests as well!'

The butler strode down the corridor and mumbled, 'It's just another pastime invented for the idle rich.'

Alice nodded. She enjoyed hearing their banter levelled against the duchess. 'Well, I've heard her ladyship tell guests that her friend, the duchess of Bedford invented the afternoon tea to cover the low point of the afternoon when women were often peckish.'

The cook exploded. 'Peckish! A family of six could live on what her and the duke eat in one day.'

They both heard steam hiss from a pan on the stove and cook swung around to rescue her potatoes.

Even though Alice would never admit this to the other staff, she actually liked her ladyship. In her early thirties, the duchess was forward thinking and always interested in new developments. She was never hesitant about expressing her opinion, and Alice knew the duke was often intimated by her. As were the rest of the family.

Alice smiled hurrying along the corridor. She also knew the duchess was kind-hearted and generous - or at least she had been to her. She reached her private look-out cupboard behind the lounge door and crouched down onto her hunkers. This is where she spied on everyone. It was her own secret place where she could dream of the time away looking at the splendour of a world in which she would never belong.

The lounge was a large square-shaped room with a high ceiling and beautiful decoration. She'd heard the duchess once explain that she liked to take low tea in this room because all of the furniture was coffee table height. Which of course, suited the blue flowered teapot, cups, saucers, milk jug, and sugar bowl, perfectly.

Alice looked at the finger cucumber sandwiches, small fancy cakes, scones, and savoury tartlets on display and licked her lips. Cook often gave the staff leftovers and she hoped they would be some today.

Two of the duchess's closet friends appeared and Alice stared at their beautiful dresses as they strutted around the lounge area. The blonde lady's dress was in a deep purple colour with cream and red trims. The red colour also matched a huge, long feather in her hat. Alice sighed knowing how long it would have taken her maid to attach the corsets and petticoats underneath.

The taller lady with black hair wore a peppermint green and polka dot dress which was full-skirted and more in-fashion. The dress gradually moved to the back of her silhouette with a narrow waist and sloping shoulders. Her hat was box-shaped with the polka dots giving it a jaunty appearance.

Alice grinned then heard cook calling her name along the corridor. Quickly, she straightened up and brushed the dust from the bottom of her drab black skirt. Well, that's my dreams over for today, she thought and scurried back along to the kitchen.

The WI Chocolate Cake Competition

'Ah, this will be about the cake stall competition next week,' Kirsty said to her husband excitedly tearing open the envelope. 'The WI are holding it in Chester-le-Street church hall so everyone can come along to buy slices of cake and have coffee. The hall is to be decked out with decorations and balloons for the kids and all the proceeds are going to the Children's Cancer North.'

She read quickly then gasped when she saw the name, Jess Richardson. 'Oh, no! It can't be!'

Matt sighed. 'Now, what?'

Kirsty re-read the letter. The WI had decided to join forces with another branch in Spennymoor. It was to be a spectacular display of cake-baking which, after all, was what the WI was famous for. To make the baking competition a little more interesting the committee had partnered ladies together from both branches in a twosome and were told which variety of cake to bake. The good news in the letter was that the chosen cake was chocolate, her speciality, but the bad news was that she'd been paired up with Jess. Just seeing the name made her heckles rise.

'I mean, out of all the women in the two branches, why, oh, why did they have to give me Jess to bake with?'

Matt shook the newspaper irritably and then his head. 'Emma, for goodness sake, grow up! It's nearly twenty years ago,' he snapped. 'Don't you think it's time to put this behind you and move on!'

Kirsty bit her lip, and she could hear her voice wobble. 'It's all right for you to say that but it wasn't you that Jess humiliated.'

Matt stood up and squeezed her shoulder heading into the kitchen. 'Look, why not be the bigger person and hold out the olive branch which will make you feel better whether it was your fault or not.'

Kirsty cried out, 'But it wasn't my fault. Jess was the one who went off with my boyfriend!'

She realised that she was shouting at the empty doorway because Matt had disappeared out into his garden shed. She let herself think back to that night. The night of the school disco and how she'd fled home in tears because her boyfriend of three weeks had gone home with Jess. But only after she had caught them snogging in the bus shelter.

Kirsty tutted remembering their friendship. They'd started Red Rose Primary School together and had been the best of friends up until the disco. And, although Jess lived near Spennymoor she'd never seen or spoken another word to her since that night.

She opened her laptop and used Jess's email address from the letter. Following Matt's advice, she tried to make the invite to her kitchen as friendly as possible. Jess answered within minutes in the same responsive tone and arrangements were made for her to come the day before the competition. This would give them plenty of time to bake the chocolate cake although Kirsty was quietly confident that her recipe would be the best. It was a tried-and-tested recipe that never failed.

The day arrived and Kirsty was in a spin. She'd changed her outfit twice settling on new jeans that were uncomfortably tight but looked good, and a clean white T-Shirt. At nearly six-foot, Kirsty had always struggled with her height and lived in flat shoes. Her make-up was carefully applied, and she stood back from the mirror smiling. This was probably the best she would ever be then grinned at Matt's wolf-whistle when she sashayed into her kitchen.

The kitchen had been newly installed last year, and Kirsty was keen to show it off to all and sundry, although she didn't know what Jess's home was like. She could live in a mansion for all she knew and sighed lifting two mixing bowls out of the drawer. In fact, she knew nothing about Jess at all. Had she married the boy from the disco, and was he a wonderful husband? Did she have children or an amazing career? Or both?

Collecting flour, cocoa powder, and sugar from the cupboard, Kirsty wondered what she looked like now. At school, Jess had been a small delicate girl with masses of blonde curly hair and huge blue eyes. She'd been petite, around five feet, and looked great in any clothes she threw on compared to Kirsty who'd been gangly, flat chested and stick thin. There'd always been a trail of boys after Jess but until the disco she had given them a wide birth feigning no interest.

Kirsty gathered eggs, butter and milk from the fridge and set out coffee mugs. Would Jess still look as pretty? Kirsty lifted her chin. Feeling jealous from losing out to Jess was irrational at her age. Matt was right, it was time she grew up and got over the schoolgirl betrayal.

Kirsty heard Matt's voice talking then laughing and she looked out of the kitchen window. He was walking up to the door with Jess.

Kirsty gasped. Jess was dressed in a blue jacket and old trainers that she could tell had seen better days. Jess had also gained weight. Gone was the amazing schoolgirl image that Kirsty had carried around in her head for years.

She pulled open the door and planted the biggest smile onto her face. 'Jess!' She cried. 'How great to see you.'

Her friend stepped gingerly into the kitchen and Kirsty pulled out a chair for her.

Matt headed back out into his shed and Jess slumped down onto the seat. 'I didn't realise it was so far from the bus stop and, well, I wasn't sure what to expect,' she said.

Kirsty took her jacket and could see Jess's face full of awe while she looked around the room.

Jess shook her curls that were now more tinged with grey than blonde. 'What a fantastic kitchen.'

Kirsty made coffee then sat down at the table. They began to talk about the WI and their lives now. She learned that Jess had suffered from ill health and lost her husband in a car accident ten years ago. She was on her own and Kirsty felt incredibly sorry for her. Kirsty knew she had been much more fortunate in life than her friend and swallowed hard at her earlier misgivings.

Draining her coffee, Kirsty explained about her recipe for the cake and showed her a photograph of one she'd made last month.

Jess nodded. 'Well, I'm happy to go along with anything because I'm not much of a baker,' she said. 'I only put my name down on the list hoping I'd be paired with someone who was a good cook. It was either this or flower arranging at another meeting,' she said and giggled.

Kirsty relaxed and smiled. She could see the teenage look back on Jess's face while they began to work together in the kitchen. Weighing out the ingredients they chatted about the cookery classes at school and laughed remembering Emma's disastrous attempt at cheese scones.

When the cake was baked to perfection, she showed Jess how to make the ganache icing and chocolate curls for the sides. They chatted like the old friends they had been and discussed what had happened to their other class members.

Kirsty knew her large hands were too clumsy to make the small chocolate decorations in fine detail and told Jess this.

Jess smiled. 'Okay, let's see what I can do,' she said, and with her nimble fingers cut out and made chocolate animal decorations to place on the top of the cake.

The cake was finished and stood proudly on the Island in the middle of the kitchen. Kirsty sighed in satisfaction. With Jess's help the cake looked great and she prayed it would win the competition.

'It looks amazing now you've made the brilliant decorations and I know it'll taste great, so, I think we are on to a winner, here.'

Jess sighed and said, 'Look, Emma, I've really enjoyed meeting up with you again, and, well, I'd just like to say I am sorry about what happened years ago at the disco.'

Kirsty took in a deep breath. There it was like the elephant back in the room after twenty years. She didn't know how to respond. Should she just wave it aside as though it had never happened and graciously accept her apology. But something inside her rebelled and she couldn't help herself. 'But why, Jess. Why would you do that to me?'

'I don't know - it just sort of happened,' she said, and her face reddened. 'I'd had too many drinks and when he pulled me outside and kissed me, my head was spinning!'

Kirsty remembered how jealous she'd felt watching them kiss and shouted, 'But he was my guy! You should have pushed him away because he wasn't yours for the taking.'

Jess swung around. 'Oh, for goodness' sake, he was a no-good waster and I only saw him a few more times then he went off to join the army,' she said. 'He meant nothing to me but what hurt more was you cutting me off, ignoring my calls, and snubbing me at the next disco. I thought we were better friends than that?'

She glared at Jess. 'And so did I!' Kirsty yelled. 'I never dreamt that you would take my boyfriend from me.'

'Oh, believe me, Emma,' Jess snarled. 'You were better off without him.'

Kirsty felt the blood pumping around her body. 'Don't you dare tell me what was for the best!' Kirsty shouted and swung her arm around in temper.

Jess called, 'Look out! Watch the cake!'

But it was too late to stop the cake crashing to the floor. Silence struck while they both stared down at the splattered cake.

Jess raised her eyebrows in the comical way that she used to do and said, 'Hmm, maybe I should have done the flower arranging.'

Kirsty shrugged her shoulders and muttered, 'Ooops!'

They burst into laughter and Kirsty felt all the anger leave her. She leaned over the countertop and laughed until tears ran down her face.

Jess threw her arms around Kirsty and hugged her. 'Oh, I've missed you,' she said.

Kirsty grinned. 'Me, too, let's not fall out again.'

Jess nodded and asked, 'So, is there time to bake another cake?'

Kirsty shook her head. 'Nope, I haven't anymore ingredients.'

Jess jumped up. 'Come on, we'll have to do what the Calendar Girls did,' she said. 'Do you drive?'

Kirsty nodded and grabbed her jacket following Jess out of the kitchen. She giggled as they hurried to the car and called out, 'Well, I'm not stripping off my clothes for a photograph!'

'Noooo,' Jess said. 'We're going to M&S to buy a chocolate cake!'

She Had to See Him

Grace ambled through the doors into Heathrow Airport. Going home to Newcastle usually filled her with excitement. She loved looking down from the aeroplane at The Tyne Bridge, but now she bit her lip. This time she wouldn't be breezing in and saying, 'Hi, I'm home.'

Grace sighed, but it had to be done.

Glancing up at the board she gave a small cry of alarm when she saw, CANCELLED, next to her flight. She raced to the check-in desk where an attendant told her there'd been technical problems and the next flight was the following morning.

'But that'll be too late,' she cried. 'I have to see him before that!'

Grace slumped down on a seat pulling out her mobile. There was a train in two hours, and she raced outside into the taxi queue. She tried to ring him but got his voicemail.

In the taxi, Grace tried to quell her churning stomach. She wasn't the best traveller on trains, and it was a knocking bet she was going to be sick.

Three people were in front of her at the information desk in Kings Cross Station and when she approached the LNER counter the assistant shook his head. 'Sorry, all the tickets are sold now - the train is full.'

Grace cried, 'But it can't be!' Tears welled up in her eyes. 'Look, can't you squeeze one more passenger in - I have to see him!'

He tutted. 'No, Madam, that's against regulations but I can get you on a train in the morning?'

She caught a small sob and stepped back. 'N...no, that'll be too late – it will be all over by then.'

She stood still willing herself not to burst into hysterical sobbing.

A teenager who had been in front of her in the queue said, 'Why not try the over-night coach - you'll be there by five in the morning.'

Grace smiled her thanks. Once more she hurried outside and into another taxi which eventually deposited her at Victoria coach station.

Clutching a coach ticket firmly in her hand she sat in a greasy-spoon café and sent him a text, 'Flight is cancelled, train is full, but I'm coming on overnight coach. I will be there – don't do anything until I get there at 5am!'

Settled in her seat on the coach, Grace sighed. If her travel arrangements had gone to plan the flight would be landing now at Newcastle airport. And that would have given her time to talk to him. To explain what she'd seen.

And, if she'd been ten minutes earlier at the train station, she'd be roaring her way up the east coast to him right now. How and why had everything gone pear-shaped? Grace thought of her gran who would say, maybe it's just not meant to be – it's the universe telling you not to do this.

When the lights on the coach went out, Grace closed her eyes and tried to sleep - she couldn't. The thought of the wedding arrangements that would all come tumbling down around their ears made her stomach lurch. But it had to be done. She couldn't live through a lie. The dishonesty would drive her crazy.

Suddenly, the coach came to a jolt and stopped. Other passengers around her began to moan when the driver explained about the flat tyre and how they'd have to be transferred to another coach. The delay could add another two hours onto the journey. Grace let the tears slide down her face. Perhaps her gran was right because something was definitely trying to stop her from reaching him.

When the new coach arrived and sped off trying to make up for lost time, Grace cried herself into a troubled sleep. Her dreams were full of smashed wedding cakes, torn and disfigured white dresses, wedding presents to be returned and weeping relatives.

The noise of passengers collecting their luggage from overhead racks woke her with a jolt and she looked out of the window to see her dad waiting on John Dobson Street outside Newcastle Library. Standing next to him was Joe.

She recognised his curly dark brown hair and big blue eyes. Even at a distance she could see the apprehension and wariness in those eyes. The eyes of a man who had always trusted her. Grace gulped, knowing she was going to shatter all of that in one fell swoop.

She took a deep breath just as the sun came up and climbed into the back of her dads car. Grace grasped Joe's hand and told him quietly exactly what she'd seen.

He took the news better than what she'd thought he would. She watched him pick at the skin on his thumb nail like she'd done a thousand times.

'Joe,' she whispered. 'I'm so very sorry, but I couldn't let you marry her without knowing. You're my little brother and I'd never forgive myself if I hadn't told you.'

Milking Day in Wooler

The milking room is noisy today, Tom thinks. He shuffles around with his stick looking at the healthy clean cows who are mooing and snorting. The machinery is clanging on the milking units in stainless steel which are spotlessly clean. He can see his face reflected in them and smiles.

His son, Michael is in the corner of the shed. He's tall, strong limbed, with dark hooded eyes. Tom thinks, it's like looking at his younger self in a mirror.

He doesn't need to oversee milking now because Michael is in control. He's just like he had been at twenty-seven. Farming is in his blood and Tom knows he loves every day, he's a chip off the old block.

Michael hurries over to him. 'Why didn't you stay in bed with your cuppa,' he says. 'I've got this now.'

Tom nods. In his younger days, he'd longed to lie in bed but now that he could he still woke at five every morning. 'I know you have, Son'

Michael had said last week. 'I want to buy another business from a nearby farm who make cream cheese. They buy the milk from us anyway, so it makes sense. And because the supermarkets are driving milk prices down, we need another revenue just in case. The profit on cream cheese is great. It might need a little investment, but it'll be worth it in the long run.'

He'd heard his late wife, Jeanie saying, we shouldn't have all our eggs all in one basket,

Tommy, and he had smiled. She'd called him Tommy from the day they met, and he still missed her dreadfully.

He had signed their farm near Wooler over to Michael three years ago. But his son's words, a little investment, had made Tom's stomach churn. However, his decisions were the future of the farm and there hadn't been a flicker of uncertainty in Michael's eyes. All Tom had said was, 'Well, I suppose you know what you're doing.'

Tom wished Michael would meet a nice girl and settle down to have a family. He looked around the shed now. It had been different in his day when his father had taught him to milk. There hadn't been all the paperwork and fancy equipment. Michael calls it, state of the art, whatever that's supposed to mean. He frowns, but why cream cheese?

A female voice from the yard calls out, 'Yoo-hoo, Michael...'

Michael hasn't heard with all the noise, so he hobbles outside. Some days the arthritis was worse than others. A young woman is there with the back of her small van open. Inside are three big tubs and one has the lid off.

The sign on the van says, 'Johnsons Cream Cheese'

Ah, this must be Steve Johnsons gal. He never had sons just two girls and Tom remembers his wife; she was a stunner. Not as beautiful as his Jeanie was, but there again none were, he'd had the best girl in the whole of Northumberland.

This woman is pretty like her mam. She's slim, with brown curly hair around a pixie face. Her blue eyes are shining, and her cheeks are rosy red with being outdoors all day. It's nice to think she's stayed on the farm and not left to work in Wooler and Alnwick like many of the young people do now. Tom knows how lucky he is that Michael didn't and has always wanted to farm. But there again, who wouldn't? It is Northumberland and the best rural county in the North East.

I wander over and look at the tubs.

She smiles shyly at me. 'Em, I was looking for Michael?'

He fits the pieces together and chuckles. Ah, so this is his interest in cream cheese.

'Do you want to try some,' she asks. 'It's made from your milk?'

He nods and she scoops a spoonful out of the tub then holds it to him. He takes the spoon and puts it into his mouth. It's clean, fresh, and very smooth as he rolls it around his tongue.

'That's delicious,' he says. 'It'll be lovely on Jacobs cream crackers.'

Michael bounds out of the milking shed behind him. 'Hey there, Hannah, pleased you could make it.'

She smiles and he grins at her. Tom can see their eyes lock together. It's how he always looked at Jeanie. He decides to retreat and wanders over to the farmhouse thinking of her name, Hannah.

In the kitchen he tidies up breakfast dishes because Michael might want to bring her in for a cuppa. He walks to the old dresser and stares at the photograph of Jeanie then strokes his roughened thumb down the photograph. 'She's called, Hannah,' he whispers. 'She seems like a lovely lass and I'm sure everything will be fine for him now.'

Cruising Into a New Life

I take a big deep breath and look in the long mirror in the bathroom. I'm in a single cabin onboard a cruise ship which left North Shields dock a few days ago. I shake my head at the image before me. It doesn't look anything like me. Well, not the old Geraldine Thompson. I smile. This Geraldine Thompson who left St. Nicholas Psychiatric Unit six days ago looks completely different now. Inside and out.

I'm not the old Geraldine who was frumpy, overweight, with long greyish hair scrapped back into a sever bun. I'd worn black or brown two-piece suits with thick tights and grey shirts all my adult life. My mam's friend, Mrs Whittaker who is a dressmaker had made them exactly to Mam's instructions - not mine. I'd never had a choice of clothing with Mrs Whittaker. Nor a choice of footwear. My feet had been forever in brown flat brogues or laced up boots.

I smile now and smooth down the sides of the white pencil skirt and spin around to look at my back. I chuckle. The navy silk blouse is tight fitting and shows off all my curves in just the right places.

I feel the slight sway of the ship as it comes into dock. I know the routines of cruising because I've been on many before but always sharing a cabin with mam. This time I've loved having the cabin all to myself.

Grinning, I peer closer into the mirror at my face. My hair has been cut in a short trendy style and coloured a rich auburn. It's shining with the sun flooding through the balcony window. And I'm wearing makeup for the first time in my life.

Mam had never approved of make-up. She'd once snarled at me, 'You'll look like a harlot!'

A fellow patient in St. Nicholas called, Jeanie had shown me how to apply the rich face cream and foundation. We'd giggled practising how to sweep blusher across my cheeks. And with all the weight I've lost playing tennis and not eating Mam's stodgy puddings, I actually have cheekbones now. I run the tip of my tongue around my front teeth to make sure the red lipstick hasn't marked them. I can't resist a small hoot imaging Mam's face and comments about hussies who wear bright red lipstick.

I place the jaunty blue hat on the back of my head and swish my hair from side to side making sure it is securely fastened. I don't want it to blow off on my descent down the gangway.

After sailing for a few days where I've stayed mainly in my cabin, we are docking in Norway today and I can feel my insides bubble with excitement.

The water is gently lapping on the sides of the ship as staff hurriedly lower and secure the metal gangway. I wait in the queue patiently taking big breaths of fresh sea air then follow the man in front who is wearing a white sun hat. He reaches the railings and stands to the side allowing me to go first. I smile my thanks to him and take my first step.

Now that it is time to disembark my stomach lurches and my heart begins to thump. The old feelings of poor mental health with a low self-esteem, no confidence and depressing thoughts fly into my mind. I can't do this. I want to shout, this isn't me. I'm dressed up to look like somebody else. My mam's constant haranguing drones on and on in my ears.

My head drops and I look down. I'd forgotten about my new shoes, and I stare at them. The shoes are white with a two-inch heel and a brown toe-covering. They are simply gorgeous, and I smile. Out of my whole transformation it is the shoes that make the biggest difference.

I hear Doctor Jones words from a song in my mind. 'Step out, Geraldine, you can do this, walk tall and meet the world right in the eye.'

His words batter out my mam's drone firmly from my mind. I lift my head up and place my hand on the rail to make my descent.

I stride confidently down the first two steps. Out of the corner of my eye I see the man dip his hat. He has a lovely smile and kind sparkling blue eyes.

He asks, 'How have we been on board for days and I've never met you?'

My heart soars and I stifle down a giggle. 'Ah, I've been in hiding,' I tease and tilt my head to the side.

'Well let me put that right straight away,' he says taking my arm and guiding me down to the end of the gangway.

His arm is just the extra reassurance I need. I smile up at him happily look forward to my adventure in Norway.

Fairy on a Toadstool

I'm sitting on a big ceramic toadstool in Mr Thompson's garden which is in a place called, Hexham. I'd heard him tell his neighbour that he'd bought the toadstool at the garden centre. Being a fairy, I'm not exactly sure what a centre is, but I do like the toadstool. It has an orange top and is smooth under my little legs. I smooth down my green taffeta skirt and tuck my feet into the hem.

I've been in Mr Thompson's garden for a while now because it's a nice place to hang out and will probably stay here forever. Happy fairies like nice places.

However, I'm a little concerned because I haven't seen Mr Thompson for a few days now. Usually I hear his whistle every morning opening the garden shed. In fact, that's where I first met him. In the shed. It had been dark inside and because I can control and project light into places, I'd done just that.

He'd gasped when he saw me sitting between his watering can and tub of tomato feed. 'What the hell!' He'd shouted.

I'd fluttered my big green wings in a greeting. 'Hi, there,' I'd whispered. 'If you can see me then you'll be blessed with good luck and happiness.'

He'd rubbed his eyes and blinked as though he couldn't believe what he was seeing then stumbled backwards out of the shed.

I'd grinned because I'm a bit of a shock to people, but over the months we've got to know each other. He looks out for me now wherever I choose to settle. Today it's the toadstool.

I make a little garland of daisies by twirling the stems around each other and place it on top of my blonde curly hair. I would be feeling mischievous and full of fun today if it wasn't for the fact that Mr Thompson still hasn't arrived.

My long black antennae start to twitch, and I know someone is coming towards the back of the garden. It's Mrs Thompson. I watch her sit on the garden bench and talk into a small machine that she is holding onto her ear. Even at this distance I can hear another voice.

'Oh, Mam, let's hope he's better today. I wish I could be there with you, but I can't leave the kids and drive up the country!'

I watch Mrs Thompson dab her eyes with a white lace handkerchief and pull her shoulders back. 'Now, Penny,' she says. 'Don't you worry about me, I'm fine. I've to ring the hospital at lunchtime to find out how your dad is doing.'

My heart starts to flutter, and I straighten out my legs over the toadstool. Oh, no, Mr Thompson is ill and at the hospital. I know Penny is his daughter because he's told me all about her. And, how their son died in a car accident four years ago at the market place in front of Hexham Abbey. He talks a lot about him.

This poor woman, I think and fly over to her. I perch on the arm of the bench just as she clicks off the machine. Now I know why I've been hanging around for so long - Mrs Thompson needs me to restore her emotions and low spirits.

I see her staring at me. Her whole face lights up and she grins then clicks her tongue. 'Well, I never, Bill told me we had a fairy at the bottom of the garden, but I just laughed. I thought he was teasing me.'

'No,' I smile. 'He wasn't - I'm here and want to help.'

Her big blue eyes fill with tears.

I whisper, 'Mr Thompson told me you had lovely eyes and how they were the first thing he fell in love with.'

She leans forwards now and sobs into her handkerchief.

'Mrs Thompson, if you can see me then you have three wishes,' I say. 'Tell me what they are?'

Mrs Thompson sniffles and dries her eyes. 'I wish Bill was better. I wish Bill could get over the flu. I wish my Bill was at home with me.'

I spread my wings knowing there is much work to be done and fly off into the sky.

Later that day as I return to the toadstool, I see Mrs Thompson rush outside with the machine on her ear again.

'Penny! Oh, Penny,' she cries. 'Your dad is much better, and the nurse reckons if he continues to make good progress, he could be home by the end of the week!'

The Beautician Comes to Stay

Deborah couldn't believe the words her daughter-in-law, Zoe whispered into her mobile. 'But she's spying on me, Simon! She's watching every move I make.'

'Well, really!' Deborah muttered to herself and stomped out into the garden. She headed over to the summerhouse and slumped down in the wicker rocking-chair then sighed. Now she was being accused of spying and in her own home.

She tutted and thought back over the weekend. Had she said something to upset Zoe? The last thing she wanted was to be thought of as the dragon mother-in-law, but she couldn't understand what was going wrong between them.

Granted, with living in Jesmond and them being near London she hadn't spent much time in Zoe's company, but on the few occasions they had got along well together. So, what was the problem now they were staying with her?

She thought back to six weeks ago when Simon had rang.

'I've good news, Mam. I'm getting a promotion at work and transferring from the London branch up to Newcastle. So, we've bought a new-build house just a few miles away from you and I wondered if we could stay until the new house is ready. It'll be two months at the most.'

Deborah had wanted to whoop with happiness thinking of them coming to stay and had cried, 'Of course! It'll be fantastic to

have you all and I'll make over the single
room into a nursery for Evie.'

Now, she saw Zoe carrying Evie out into
the garden and calling, 'Deborah...'

Scrambling up out of the chair she hurried
to meet her. 'I'm here,' she said. 'I was just
enjoying the evening sun.'

'Oh, right, could you keep an eye on Evie
for me, while I get ready to go out. I just
need a quick shower and hair wash.'

Deborah looked down at her granddaughter
and was rewarded with a big sloppy smile.
She melted on the spot. 'Yes, of course, give
her to me until bed-time.'

'Thanks,' Zoe said. 'Simon should be home
in an hour to get ready for the party.'

Deborah watched her long thin legs in
shorts skipping back down the garden. 'Look
at her,' she whispered. 'Your Mam's not
much more than a lass herself.'

Evie gurgled in reply and as Deborah
rocked the chair, she was asleep in minutes.
Zoe was bright, with a cheerful disposition
which considering what she'd been through,
was commendable. She was kind and
thoughtful especially to Simon who she
obviously adored.

Deborah closed her eyes and remembered
their whirlwind romance. The first time she'd
even heard of Zoe was the day Simon
brought her home on Christmas Eve.

'We're going to get married next year when
Zoe finishes her beautician's course at
college,' he'd said. 'And I know Zoe is
younger than me, but she is quite mature.

She's had to be really because her parents were killed in the 2005 London bombings.'

He'd lifted his shoulders and his face had glowed with pride. 'She's lived with an aunt in London since then and found work in a local beautician's salon until the course starts.'

Of course, Deborah had felt incredibly sorry for Zoe and couldn't begin to imagine what she'd been through, but her main concern had been Simon.

She'd seen that look on his face many times as a boy when he'd brought waif and strays home wanting to protect them. She'd prayed this wasn't the case with Zoe because feeling sorry for someone was a lot different to being in love with them.

However, the wedding had been brought forward because Zoe was pregnant, and she'd left her beauticians course to be a full-time Mother.

The late sun casted a glow on Evie's chubby cheeks, and she smiled down at her. She knew most women thought their grandchildren were beautiful, but Evie was especially so, she looked just like Zoe.

Deborah bit her lip. How could she make things better between them? She'd offered to help with shopping, cooking, and looking after Evie, but Zoe obviously saw this as interference or spying, as she called it. Deborah sighed, of course, she'd never expected the special close relationship that mothers have with their daughters, but she had hoped they would have at least become friends.

She rested her head back on the chair and looked around the summerhouse knowing it needed another coat of paint. It was the same as all of the old house now - in need of updating. Her friends advised her to move into a small flat or bungalow but she loved the location of her home just off Osbourne Road with good links into the city. And, Jesmond Dene Park was one of her favourite places to walk.

It was nearly ten years since her husband, Jack had died and afterwards the smell of his cigars had lingered in the summerhouse. Jack had thought she didn't know about the sly cigars he smoked in there, but she did, which still made her smile. She wondered what he would have thought about their troubles. She mused, he'd probably tell her to keep going and persevere.

Before they'd arrived, she had made a big effort and transformed the single bedroom in pretty pinks for Evie as a nursery. And along with her friends at the Thai Chi class, she'd poured over interior design magazines. Together they had chosen cream colours and a vibrant gold-patterned wallpaper in Simon's old bedroom. She had bought a new sleigh bed and all the soft furnishings and lamps matched perfectly. Zoe had gasped in delight when she'd first walked into the room. 'Oh, Deborah, it's beautiful!'

Later, as she tip-toed out of the nursery she heard Zoe give a loud wail.

'But, Simon, you promised! I don't want to go on my own. It's going to be all couples tonight and I don't want to sit there feeling like a spare part.'

Deborah stopped still and heard Zoe start to cry. It sounded so pitiful. She peered around the bedroom door to see tears rolling down her cheeks. Her usual flawless complexion was covered in big red blotches.

'Zoe,' she said. 'Whatever's the matter?'

Zoe swung around in surprise. 'I'll tell you what the matter is, Deborah, it's your wonderful son. He makes promises but never keeps them!'

'Oh, dear,' she murmured stepping towards her.

Zoe jumped up from the bed and scoffed. 'Of course, you won't want to listen to me slagging off your, *golden boy,* will you?'

Deborah took a deep breath. 'I haven't said that Zoe and I'm sure he's not a saint, but I'd like to help?'

'Well, he's got to work late again and probably won't make it to the party in Newcastle. He still wants me to go but I'm sick of going to things on my own,' she wailed. 'A…and things have changed since Evie was born because I've put on a little weight so maybe he doesn't fancy me anymore?'

Zoe slumped down onto the bed, buried her face in her hands and began to sob. Deborah made a quick decision and put an arm along

Zoe's shoulders. 'Now, now, there's no need for all this upset,' she soothed. 'You're just letting your imagination run riot.'

Suddenly, Zoe threw herself into Deborah's arms and laid her head on her chest. Deborah wrapped both her arms around her daughter-in-law and held her tightly in a big hug.

Zoe looked up at her with swollen eyes. 'Do you think so? It's just that I'm worried he's going off me and we're drifting apart?'

'What absolute rubbish!' Deborah said. 'He's totally besotted with both of you.'

'D…do you really think so?'

Deborah smiled. 'I'm certain. And even though he is my *golden boy*, I'll certainly be having words with him. Work or not, he shouldn't neglect you like this.'

Zoe snivelled into tissues. 'You will,' she said. 'But I thought you didn't like me?'

'Now, where on earth did you get that idea from. How could I possibly not like someone who loves *golden boy* as much as I do, and who has given us Evie?'

'Oh, Deborah, I do love him heaps.'

'I know you do,' she said. 'Now, stop crying because you're making a mess of your lovely face.'

Deborah slackened her arms to pull away, but Zoe snuggled-in closer.

'I used to sit like this with my mum, Deborah. When she hugged me, it felt like I'd suffocate, but it was where I always felt safe,' she said. 'You often remind me of her and if she'd been here, I'm sure you would have liked her.'

Deborah's throat tightened and tears stung the back of her eyes. She remembered when Simon was born and although she'd been much older, she knew how scared and vulnerable she had felt. Being a new mam wasn't easy and not only was Zoe coping with Evie she was doing it all without her own mother.

'From what you've told me, Zoe, I think we'd have got along really well. And I know she would have been proud of you.'

'Oh, do you think so?'

Deborah smiled. 'I'm certain of it.'

She smelt a fruity aroma from Zoe's long blonde hair. 'What is that shampoo you use; it smells gorgeous.'

Zoe stretched over to the dressing table. 'It's a salon shampoo from where I used to work. It makes such a difference to the condition of your hair. You can borrow some if you want to?'

'Oh, thanks, I'll try it,' she said. 'I'm afraid I still use the same shampoo I did when I was younger. My mam used to buy a big bottle for the whole family.'

'Really?' Zoe asked. 'But everyone couldn't have had the same type of hair? I mean, what if someone had greasy hair and another had dry?'

Deborah burst out laughing. 'Well, it wouldn't have made any difference, because there weren't different types of shampoo back then. But my mam used to give my hair a final rinse with vinegar to bring out the shine.'

'Vinegar!' Zoe exclaimed. 'Not conditioner?'

They both giggled and Deborah sat next to her in front of the dressing table.

Zoe peered closely into the mirror. 'I could fix my face if I decide to go to the party.'

'Well, I think you should. I'm here to look after Evie and you'll enjoy yourself once you get there.'

Zoe smoothed moisturiser onto her face and in circles around her eyes.

Picking up the pot of moisturiser, Deborah spread a little on her hand marvelling at the lightness compared to her old pot of thick cream. She said, 'This is lovely.'

Zoe grinned. 'Try it to see if it makes a difference, although you do have incredibly good skin, Deborah, for your age.'

She peered into the mirror. 'Mmm, maybe it is time for a change?'

Zoe applied her foundation and Deborah watched fascinated at her confidence and style.

She smiled. 'It's such a shame you had to leave the beauticians course, it's obvious you have a natural flair,' she said. 'But, if ever you want to go back, I'd look after Evie for you.'

They both jumped when the back door slammed shut. Simons loud voice boomed up the stairs. 'Hey! Where are my three favourite lasses?'

Deborah smiled fondly at her daughter-in-law. 'Oh, great, here's Simon. So, Cinderella, you shall go to the ball.'

Zoe ran out onto the landing and whispered down the stairs, 'Ssshh, you'll wake Evie!'

She turned and smiled. 'Thanks, Deborah and when Evie is a little older, I might consider doing that course.'

'Yes, you should. Now off you go and have a good time.'

Zoe pulled a comical face. 'Come-on, we'd better see if *golden boy* wants to be fed before we go out.'

Laughing together, Deborah hooked an arm through Zoe's as they headed downstairs.

The Fosters in Blanchland

'But, Tom, I can't marry the bishop, he's an old man!'

Tom Foster looked at his sister, Dorothy, and sighed. She wasn't the prettiest woman in the area by any means, but certainly not the ugliest, by a long shot. She took after their mam and had a gentle kind nature.

'He might well be, Dotty, but as The Bishop of Durham, he's a very rich old man,' he said. 'And who's to know if you'll ever get another proposal?'

Dorothy smiled warmly at him and especially at his pet name for her. 'It's a good job you're my brother, Tom Foster, because I know that last comment wasn't meant with any malice.'

He nodded and gave her his cheeky-chappy smile. The smile that set hearts beating of the young girls in the village. Although he was yet to marry any of them.

Their parents had died young and the whole of Blanchland in 1684 with its eleven farms and cottages, belonged to them now. Their farmhouse was the largest in the area and Dorothy ran it with a good head for figures and the high standards mam had taught her.

***

Two years later, when the bishop returned once more and proposed again, Dorothy had an older head on her shoulders and knew that Tom had been right. She'd never had another proposal. Tom thought it an honour that she'd been singled out amongst all the women he could marry in Durham. And, yet he'd chosen her.

She'd nodded in agreement while serving the bishop his tea. Now, she looked at the older man in a new light. Dorothy noted his chubby cheeks, wrinkly neck, and his small eyes. All she'd been able to see before was his forty-year difference to her. But now, she saw the gold shimmer in the big chain lying on his tunic which distracted her from the wrinkles. The benevolence in his small eyes. And decided that the healthy diet she could impose in his house would soon get rid of his chubbiness.

'Yes, Bishop, I will marry you,' she said to Tom's obvious delight.

***

Unfortunately, no matter how hard Dorothy tried there were never any children and by the time she reached her fortieth birthday she was unwell. The bishop brought one doctor after another but sadly they all told the same story. Dorothy wasn't long for this world. Her husband prayed day and night along with their parishioners in Durham who had taken Dorothy to their hearts. But sadly, the lord took her one night and the bishop wept.

Tom arrived and the two men sat by her bedside in devastation that she'd been taken from them.

'I still can't believe she's gone,' Tom said and bit down hard on his bottom lip.

The bishop nodded and croaked, 'M…me, neither. I've loved her for so long my life won't be the same without her.'

Tom kicked at the dry mud on his boots. 'Although I'm pleased in a way because she won't see where I'm headed now,' he mumbled. 'The lord has saved her from visiting me in prison.'

The bishop looked at him and raised an eyebrow. 'What's happened?'

Tom slowly told him about the debt that had mounted up without Dotty balancing their books and his cheeks flushed when he admitted his addiction to the ale in the local pub. 'I haven't a penny to my name now,' he said. 'I wish the lord would take me rather than face my old age in prison.'

The bishop grunted. 'Leave it with me and I'll see what I can do,' he said then stood up and shook Tom's hand. 'Dorothy wouldn't let you be arrested, so I'll honour my darling wife's last wishes.'

Within months the bishop had set up, The Lord Crewe Trust and bought all of Tom's debt and remaining assets. The proceeds of monthly rents from the village and surrounding area were designated to support poor clergymen in the Northeast.

Tom Foster would have danced a jig if he'd been able to on the day that he was proclaimed debt-free. The thought of going to prison amongst criminals and murderers at his age had terrified him.

He crawled into bed that night and smiled in satisfaction. He'd known it was a good idea for Dorothy to marry the bishop, and he'd been proven right.

***

To this day, the village of Blanchland and all the farms still belongs to this trust. No one can buy their properties and everyone, even the pub and hotel, pay rent to The Lord Crewe Trust.

Turn Left or Right

I've left my flat in Whitley Bay and am walking down to the seafront. After six torturous months of breaking up with my partner, I finally feel free. The sun is shining as I swing my beach bag loving the warmth on my face.

I pass by small hotels, B&B's, bars and restaurants which hold memories of night's out with my friends. The Playhouse theatre is on my right where I've enjoyed some great productions with my family, especially Christmas pantomimes. Eventually, I arrive at the beach area and the newly refurbished Spanish City where I'd taken Mam and Dad for their favourite fish and chip anniversary lunch.

I walk across the road and look up at huge white pavilion-like structure noting the seafront area is quiet because school holidays haven't begun. It's only ten in the morning and I stop at the small café to buy a sandwich and juice.

Moving on down to the sand, I stand still in a dither. Should I turn left, or right? Often the right side of the beach is quieter but I decide to turn left for a change. Walking onto the beach I drape my large beach towel down near the water's edge. Seagulls swoop and squark while multicoloured parasols and stripy deck chairs of all colours are scattered along the beach making it look like an old-fashioned picture postcard.

In my red spotty bikini, I cover myself in suncream and toast myself in the sun for thirty minutes. Unable to resist the sea any longer, I paddle into the small waves at the sea edge. I gasp at the cold North Sea which even though the sun is blazing at twenty degrees never seems to get warm. I remind myself it's not the Mediterranean and giggle. The cool water feels lovely on my hot legs, and I wade further out to waist height laughing with delight.

I face the sand now and stare at the hotels, blocks of flats, and shops which form a dramatic back drop to our coastline. It's such a long time since I came down to the beach, I'd forgotten how much I love being here.

However, on the way out of the sea I feel a sharp sting in the side of my big toe and yelp.

A man stops next to me and asks, 'You, okay?'

I lift my foot out of the sea to see a broken shell stuck into my toe. I pull out the shell and a small trickle of blood mixes in with the small bubbly waves.

'I think so,' I say.

He puts out his arm. 'Look, hang on to me and walk on your heel back up in the sand.'

When I reach my towel, I plonk down and find an Elastoplast in my bag. After applying it, I look up at him for the first time.

I gasp in awe at the sight. He is gorgeous. He's like the handsome type of guy you would see on Baywatch not on our Whitley Bay beach.

'I'm, Sam,' he says and dazzles me with his smile.

We stay on the beach all afternoon and talk for hours. He collects cans of Coke for us, and I share my sandwich with him. Four girls in skimpy bikinis arrive and deposit their belongings in a circle near us. They laugh and take selfies of each other.

A shiver of alarm runs up my back. My ex had what everyone calls, a roving eye and had cheated on me twice in the three years we'd been together. I look around and know for certain he would have been transfixed by the girls' antics, as every other guy on the beach seemed to be. Well, everyone except Sam.

He is ignoring them and staring at me, and only me. I appear to be the subject of his focus and sigh with relief. It's going to be a long time before I put my trust in a man again but somehow deep inside, I know that Sam could be the person to help me through this.

By the time we leave the beach and walk past The Spanish City, I feel like I've known him all my life. I watch as people saunter away from the beach and bless my decision to turn left. If I'd turned right, I would never have met Sam. And that would have been regrettable because this has been, quite simply, a day in my life that I'll never forget.

Bobbing for Apples

'But I can only make so much jam, chutney, and pies with all the apples,' Maggie said to her friend, Jean. 'There seems to be more than ever this year!'

Jean sipped her coffee. 'That's true.'

Maggie got up and walked to her kitchen window. The two big apple trees that her late husband, John had lovingly cared for were laden with apples. She imagined him shaking the branches until the apples fell to the ground, and in his later days when his mobility was restricted, how she'd followed him around collecting the apples in her wicker basket.

'What am I going to do with them,' she sighed. 'These are the *D'Arcy Spice* variety which John bought from an orchard when we were first married in Durham. They're usually best picked in November, but I read online that apples are ripening two to three weeks early this year.'

Jean's eyes brimmed with empathy. 'Don't worry, we'll think of something,' she said. 'Now, come on, let's go or we'll be late for the book club.'

As they left her cottage, Maggie gazed wistfully at the fallen apples knowing she would have to collect them later - it would have upset John if she left them to rot.

In Durham Library, Maggie perched on a stool next to the headmistress from the local school, Ms Dowson.

Maggie listened and smiled at her strait-laced disposition which was renowned.

'Gosh, what a week it's been - I've never stopped! I'm trying to organise a Halloween party for the children up at the hall.'

'Up at Beamish Hall?' Maggie asked, her interest was piqued. 'How come?'

Ms Dowson folded her arms and tutted. 'Well, we're waiting for our roof in the school hall to be fixed and it's not safe to use. So, Beamish have offered me their big room to host the party.'

'Oh, right,' Maggie smiled. 'And do the family realise what they've let themselves in for?'

Ms Dowson nudged Maggie in the ribs. 'Ha! They haven't a clue – but it's taking me ages to arrange the games and prizes!'

'Well, I wouldn't know how to help with games,' Maggie said thoughtfully and bit the inside of her cheek.

Ms Dowson furrowed her thick eyebrows. 'Not so, Maggie, I remember your daughter winning best costume as a wicked witch and Jean's boy was runner up as a ghost.'

Maggie grinned. 'Oh, yes, I remember sewing that costume.'

'A local Durham farmer has donated pumpkins and my history teacher is sorting that out,' she said. 'But the other games are proving a challenge.'

Maggie remembered the fun her daughter and friends always had and how she'd come home drenched from bobbing for apples. She grinned. 'Well, I can help with the apples – I've a garden full.'

Ms Dowson clapped her chubby hands together. 'Splendid, so I'll pencil you in to organise bobbing-for-apples.'

***

The night arrived. Jean and Maggie stood to the side of the beautiful high-ceilinged room at Beamish Hall. The elegant furniture had been covered and pushed against the walls of the room to make space for the games. Ms Dowson walked around raising her voice and shouting out instructions while ticking off a list on her clipboard.

Ghostly music played from an old sound system. With the gold wallpaper around the room and big glistening chandelier, Maggie thought the room and atmosphere suited Halloween perfectly.

Different sections of the room had groups of children waiting for certain games. The scooping out of pumpkins took place with the history teacher supervising candles. Trick and treat jars were strategically located for small prizes with a little platform holding three trophies for the main prizes.

Ms Dowson called Maggie to the centre of the room where her three wicker baskets full of apples stood. A man, who looked like a gardener, arrived with an old zinc bath and placed it on the floor. Then two women arrived carrying buckets full of cold water. These were tipped into the bath and Maggie smiled wondering where the old bath had come from.

The women left and returned another twice filling the bath up to a few inches from the rim. With Ms Dowson's nod of her head, Maggie threw around thirty apples into the water amidst shrieks of laughter from the children who formed an orderly queue to bob.

The irregular shaped apples bobbed on the surface of the water with their yellow-green and reddish-brown colours glistening in the water. The apples looked their best and the fun began.

Maggie felt Jean slip her arm around her waist and squeeze her. They watched the children laugh, gurgle and shriek then munch on the apples afterwards. And, Maggie knew John would have loved to see his apples being enjoyed by the children on Halloween especially at Beamish Hall.

Black Magic on Halloween.

'You've cast a spell on me,' crooned Nina Simone from the CD. Tears rolled down Rosie's cheeks and she brushed them aside with the back of her hand. She sipped her wine and wished she could cast a spell to make him see sense and come back to her.

Rosie closed her eyes and imagined him sailing through the door. With his dark brown hair and bushy eyebrows that he'd often wiggle to make her laugh. His piercing green eyes which would bore into her especially when he wanted her. If only he would come back.

'I'm sorry, darling,' he'd say looking sheepishly at her. 'I've made a huge mistake - it's you I really love. Can you ever forgive me?'

She sighed knowing she'd forgive anything if only she could make him leave the blonde secretary.

She'd met Jack at a Halloween party in Pity Me, just outside Durham. Her face had been in a bowl of water ducking for apples and when she came up for breath he'd been in front of her laughing. He had eased her aside and stuck his face into the bowl then re-surfaced moments later triumphant with an apple between his teeth. 'This has always been my favourite night of the year,' he'd said shaking his wet fringe and laughing.

They'd been inseparable from that first night up until last Christmas when he suddenly announced that he was moving out.

Rosie poured another glass of wine as a text popped onto her mobile. Immediately her heart leapt. Was it from Jack? Her shoulders dropped when she read the name, Chrissie. It was her friend checking to see if she is okay – she answered with a smiley emoji.

Last month, when she'd been in their local club, Chrissie had said, 'I've heard Jack is getting married on Halloween, and they're having the reception here in the working man's club. Apparently, Jack had said he's finally met his soul mate.'

Rosie had swallowed hard and took a deep breath. She'd tried not to show the pain and heartache which had consumed her since Jack left. The devastation that filled her every waking moment since the door slammed shut behind him.

She'd been doing a good job of pretending she couldn't care less whenever his name was mentioned. But her chin had wobbled ever so slightly, and Chrissie had pounced. 'Oh, I'm sorry, me and my big mouth! But I thought you weren't interested anymore?'

Rosie had retorted. 'Nooo, of course I'm not!'

Now, her black cat, Cordelia, jumped up onto her knee and Rosie whispered, 'Oh, why doesn't he come back home to us?'

Jack had bought Cordelia on their first anniversary. She'd gasped in delight at the black kitten with huge green eyes. Cordelia had purred loudly, and Rosie had murmured, 'Ah, Jack, she's gorgeous.'

'A black cat for my Halloween witch,' he'd said. 'And every time I look at her, I'll think of you in that costume last night!'

They'd been to a Halloween fancy-dress party in the club when she'd worn the perfect witches costume. A large cauldron filled with green punch, labelled, The Secret Potion had seemed to get stronger as the evening progressed. Jack had said, 'God, you look amazing in that costume.'

It was a long flowing dress, cut low at the front, and with the tall, pointed hat, and broomstick, she had looked sensational. They'd had such a wild night that it was quite simply something she would never forget. Every Halloween night since, he had left a box of Black Magic chocolates on her pillow.

However, today was the day. It was Halloween and his wedding day. Rosie knew she would never receive the chocolates again. He would give a box to his new wife. She gulped at her own words - his new wife.

Chrissie had said, 'Apparently, it's the only date they could arrange the wedding.'

But Rosie wasn't convinced that was the true reason. For Jack to get married on Halloween was a double whammy because it had been so special to them. She wondered if memories of their Halloween nights would be in his mind this morning, or maybe Rosie didn't even figure in his thoughts now.

She glanced at her watch knowing that in an hour he would be saying, I do. But not to her. He would be saying, I do to another woman.

Her throat tightened. She clenched her jaw and felt her cheeks burn shouting into the silence of the room. 'So, how does that work, Jack?'

He'd always told her he would never make that commitment to her, or any other woman. So why now? A vein pulsed in her temple, and she rubbed her forehead. She looked up at the shelf of photographs and smiled at one of Aunt Sybil sitting by the fire in her cottage in old Pity Me village.

Jack had once said, 'You look just like her and I'm sure you have her supernatural powers!'

Rosie had scoffed. 'Don't be silly, I don't get messages from the other side like she did.'

'Well,' he'd chortled. 'You know what I'm going to say before it actually comes out of my mouth.'

'Ah, that's only because we're so close, silly,' she'd said. 'All couples that have been together a long time do that, don't they?'

She clicked her tongue remembering the conversation and stared at the photograph. Although it was ten years since Aunt Sybil had died, and in later life she'd ended up virtually a recluse, Rosie remembered her well.

She'd often stayed with her in the cottage during her school holidays. Sybil would sit by the fire in a flowing gypsy skirt with her long-frazzled hair hanging over her face and her eyebrows drawn together staring into the flames.

The old lady had made an eerie sight, but she hadn't been afraid of her because underneath the strange character was a warm and loving aunty. The older residents of, Pity Me, had gossiped about her being a witch. But Rosie knew now that she'd just been a vulnerable old lady fixated upon the occult and black magic. Sybil had a Voodoo doll which she would often stick with pins and whisper, 'This will inflict physical harm on anyone I want revenge upon.'

And there'd been a few over the years especially her own Dad who had sailed off to Norway. 'He took a floosy with him and left your mam totally bereft,' she'd chanted sticking pins ferociously into the doll.

Rosie looked towards the dresser at her sewing basket and sighed. She didn't have an effigy or anything that would resemble such a thing. Although she did have long pins there was nothing to stick them into. She closed her eyes and tried to remember how Sybil used to chant.

Rosie cursed the blonde and hoped something would befall her as she walked into church. She thought of their local church and how the flowers would be perfect, how the bells would ring out, and how the vicar would greet them in the doorway. It had been her dream. The dream she'd had since she was a bright-eyed teenager waiting to meet her, Mr Right. She would float down the aisle in a white silk dress to meet him and everyone would turn to stare in envy at their love for each other.

Rosie ground her back teeth. But it'll be the blonde floating down the aisle to meet him now, instead of me, she seethed. The alarm on her mobile tinkled and she knew that this was the time. This was the time Jack would give himself to someone else. She squeezed her eyes tight shut wishing she had a magic wand to wave which would stop him making the biggest mistake of his life. She started to chant, 'Please don't marry her. Please come back to me. She's not right for you. I am. I always was.'

With her hands clasped together as though she was praying, she whispered, 'Oh, pleaseeeee.'

She drained the wine from her glass and her mobile rang. It was Chrissie and she croaked a shaky, 'H...Hello.'

'Hey,' Chrissie said. 'I've just grabbed the chance on my tea break to ring with the news - you'll never guess what's happened?'

Rosie took a deep breath to brace herself for details.

'Well, apparently the wedding didn't happen! Jack fell in the shower this morning and banged his head - he's unconscious in hospital.'

Rosie felt quite breathless and clutched the front of her jumper. She dropped the mobile and it landed on Cordelia's tail who leapt up from the sofa and skidded across the wood floor.

'Nooooo, no, no, it wasn't meant to happen to him,' she cried aloud.

Her heart hammered too fast. She couldn't speak. She began to sob. It was supposed to be the blonde that she cursed and not Jack. Rosie took deep breaths until she felt steadier. The thought of Jack lying unconscious, and hurt was more than she could bear. She scrambled up from the floor knowing that she must see him.

***

Within twenty minutes she was inside heading to ITU at Dryburn Hospital. Rosie knew there was a chance that the blonde would be at his bedside, but it was a risk she was willing to take because she had to explain.

She crept quietly along the corridor then heard sobbing coming from a visitor's room. Rosie spied through the crack in the door and saw the blonde talking on her mobile. That's her, she thought and sighed with relief - Jack would be alone.

Inching along the corridor looking at the names on small boards outside the cubicles, she eventually she saw his name. Slowly she eased the door open.

Rosie gasped when she saw her beloved Jack lying flat on the bed. She tiptoed forward and took his hand in hers. His skin felt cold, and she squeezed his hand hoping to convey her warmth into him.

She knew there wasn't much time and bent over to his ear. 'Jack, it's me,' she whispered. 'Please open your eyes so you can see me.'

His eyes remain closed. There was no movement. No sign that he could hear her. The thought of him never waking up made her choke back a huge sob.

She tried again. 'Jack, I didn't mean for this to happen, please forgive me!'

There was nothing but the beep of the machines next to his bed. She planted a small kiss on the corner of his mouth. A noise in the corridor reminded her that she shouldn't be there, and furtively she looked over her shoulder. She must leave now, or risk being caught.

Delving into her bag she pulled out a box of Black Magic chocolates and laid them on his pillow then crept back out of the room and fled down the corridor.

Make-Over at The Bonfire

Chloe sips her coffee and grimaces looking at the hallway. The walls are painted white, and she hates them - and that, she thinks is the first thing to go. Years ago, when they'd moved into the house in Gosforth, the wood panelling was sturdy oak, but her ex-husband, Chris had put up cheap MDF boarding in front and painted it white.

'Having the whole house painted white will look fantastic,' he'd said.

And she'd agreed. But why or how had she allowed that to happen? She loved old wood but had let him override all her likes and dislikes. Maybe in those days she'd viewed her marriage through rose-tinted glasses.

Balancing her coffee cup on the bottom stair, Chloe opens an old tool bag she has found in the garage. Choosing a small hammer and pry bar she begins to rip the sheets off. The boarding comes off without a problem and she stacks it in a pile by the front door.

Chloe wipes her hot forehead with the sleeve of her jumper. 'Phew,' she mutters but feels energised with new ideas for a complete home make-over of her house. She thinks of all the programmes on TV and repeats the slogan to herself, 'It'll be my chance to put my own stamp on the place.'

The first few months when Chris had left were hard. Her friend had said, 'You need a make-over, start at the gym and loose a little

weight then get a new hairstyle and colour –
it'll knock years off you!'

And Chloe knew her friend meant well but
she didn't want to knock years from herself.
Aged thirty three, she felt, and always had
done, quite happy with the way she was.

So, she thinks heading out of the door, there
were many types of make-overs, and she
would start with her home. After collecting
paint charts and samples of wallpapers with
vibrant colours and patterns she heads into
the corner shop.

A poster on the window advertises the
bonfire and firework display scheduled for
the following night at Gosforth Park. Chloe
chats to the shop owner, Ms Bird who suits
her name with a tiny face and rimmed
glasses perched on the end of her long thin
nose.

Chloe buys milk and hears a man's voice
behind with a strong Welsh accent.

He speaks to Ms Bird who comes over all
girly and giggly. 'Hey there,' he says, 'I'm in
charge of gathering stuff for the bonfire - any
ideas?'

Chloe spins around to face him. Although
she hasn't met him, she knew Luke had
moved into their area of Gosforth from a
neighbour and was a paramedic.

She gasps. Chloe reckons he must be well
over six foot with big shoulders and an even
bigger grin on his face. She couldn't say he
is a naturally good looking man but his eyes
are warm and friendly. She feels drawn to

him for some reason and blushes nearly as pink as Mrs Bird.

'Could you use some MDF boarding for the bonfire?' She asks. 'I've piles of it at home.'

***

Chloe opens the front door with Luke behind her and steps over the pile she'd left earlier.

'Hey that's great,' he says and picks up half of the MDF lugging it onto his shoulder. Chloe looks at his big biceps and smiles. 'I've decided to have a make-over now I'm on my own again.'

He rubs his chin. Luke reminds her of Chris when he was younger and before middle age and complacency had set in. Before their marriage had rotted. Once it had been as solid as the old oak or so she'd thought.

'Out with the old and in with the new,' Luke jokes. 'Or should I say, out with the new and back in with the old!'

She grins when he asks, 'Why not come and watch your MDF burning on the bonfire tomorrow?'

***

The beautiful display of colours in the sky makes her jaw drop. Glittering, sparkling lights explode in the dark sky around the racecourse. Chloe knows the impressive show is a sight she'll never forget. Or she muses, is it his closeness that she'll never forget?

Luke had insisted that she light the bonfire and she'd laughed watching the flames lick up the MDF panels burning brightly. And, here's to new beginnings, she'd thought.

Youngsters are squealing and running around now waving sparklers while the smell wafts across from a stall serving hot dogs. Wrapped up warm with gloves and scarf, Chloe jumps every time a banger goes off, but Luke holds securely onto her arm.

At first, Chloe had wished she was safely indoors watching from the window which is what she'd always done with Chris. But the heat and warmth from Luke's hand makes her want to stay at the bonfire more than hurry home. Chloe hopes it's a sign of good things to come.

Not Just for Christmas

Jill paced the lounge on Christmas Eve waiting for her husband, Duncan to return. Since they were married, they'd always opened one special present from each other before the kids took over Christmastime altogether. This was their time. She had lunch prepared and knew he had finished work an hour ago. Finally, she thought, at the turn of his key in the door.

Tim and Laura had started Newcastle University, so Jill knew it was going to be a little different this year. She poured glasses of wine and carried them through from the kitchen. Out of the corner of her eye she caught sight of a basket on the floor in the hall with a big red bow on the handles. Her stomach tumbled in excitement – she loved Christmas and hurried to greet him.

Duncan sat at the table looking like the proverbial cat who had got the cream. Fortunately, he loved Christmas, too and she could tell he was just as excited. She gave him a long lingering kiss and they clinked glasses. Jill had placed his gift next to the plate setting - it was a small box wrapped in red Christmas paper.

'Aaah,' he grinned. 'What have we here?'

Jill giggled and watched his surprise as he opened the box and gasped in awe at the watch. She'd seen him looking at it in Northern Goldsmith's on Northumberland Street and knew he would love the gift. Proudly, he put it onto his wrist while she tried to second guess what was in the basket. She knew it was for her.

'I'll bring the salmon,' she said hovering at the table.

Duncan took her hand. 'No, wait I have your gift in the hall.'

Jill's heart began to thump in anticipation - what present could be big enough to go in a basket?

He scurried out of the room and returned with the basket. Jill pretended she hadn't seen it and cried, 'Goodness, what on earth is this?'

She undid the bow and a small pink nose poked out of the gap. When the kitten pushed its head further out of the basket, Jill gasped.

'But it's a kitten,' she said. 'Why would you buy me a pet? We've never had them before not even when the kids were little and begged for a puppy.'

Jill's mind raced. Did he think the kitten would give her someone to look after now the kids had left and the house was quiet? She sighed. They'd already had the, empty nest, conversation. And yes, she missed them but was coping rather well.

Duncan frowned. 'D...don't you like it?'

She looked down at the kitten. It was all white with pink inner ears. It's paw pads were black and had a cute pink nose with white whiskers. Jill didn't know how to respond. She said, 'Well yes, it's adorable but I can't understand why you've bought it for me.'

'I thought the kitten would keep us company,' he said shuffling his feet.

'Ah, so you think a kitten needing my attention will fill the hole the kids have left because they don't need me any longer?'

Duncan bristled. 'No! It's not like that at all but if you don't want it, I can easily take him back to, Newcastle Dog & Cat Shelter after the holidays,' he said. 'And, the kids will always need you, Jill.'

She could see he was crushed by her reaction. 'I'm sorry,' she said cutting into her salmon. 'Let's see how we all get along.'

They began to eat lunch and the kitten crawled out of the basket under the table. She could feel it's soft fur against her legs when it purred – it felt cosy and soft.

Tim arrived shortly full of woe. 'Aww, Mam, my favourite jeans have shrunk in the washer machine at Uni,' he wailed. 'Can you do anything to save them?'

It's a good job one of his presents was two pairs of new jeans, she thought.

Laura arrived behind him in a flurry and flung herself into Jill's arms. 'My boyfriend has chucked me,' she cried. 'Where did I go wrong, Mam?'

Tim and Laura insisted she open a couple of their pressies.

Jill cried, 'But that means I'll have nothing to open in the morning!'

Not being able to refuse their pleas she opened parcels and found a food and water bowl, a litter tray, and a cat's bed. Jill knew the kids had been in on Duncan's surprise gift.

When the kitten climbed up onto her knee and she spoke softly to it, his ears pricked up with a tilt of its head on one side. Jill knew there was no question of taking the little bundle of fur back to the shelter – he'd found his new home.

The Pantomime Horse

'Why am I always at the back of the horse?' Sheila tuts and spits out a bit of fluff from the lining of the horse cover. It's okay for him at the front manoeuvring the head and legs in an upright posture with a view through the horse's eyes. But she is bent over in an uncomfortable horizontal position behind her husband with her arms around his waist.

Ian snorts. 'Because you've got the best rump, darling!'

Sheila grimaces. At one time when they were younger these funny quips would have made her giggle but after six weeks of being isolated with him at home, she can't even raise a smile.

The humorous quips were getting on her nerves. He was getting on her nerves. The large house he'd insisted they buy on Slaley Walk was getting on her nerves. It was the house he wanted to show off to friends and family. She would have been happier in the town with a small cottage in Neasham near their daughter.

She looks down through the two small holes in the bottom of the cover to see where she is putting her feet while he guides them onto the small stage. Last year she'd nearly tripped and had stumbled against his back only stopping herself from falling. Had he been concerned, not on your nelly, she sighed.

He'd been furious and hissed at her, 'Look where you're blooming well going or you'll have us both flat on our faces!'

Luckily, a little breeze floats up from the holes and she takes a deep breath to steady herself until the end of the pantomime in Darlington's church hall. If this goes according to previous years, they should only be on stage for twenty minutes. However, she seethes, this year five minutes would be too long.

She's known for a while that being close to him is a place she doesn't want to be anymore. And the last few months have reinforced her feelings. She wants to start again, and this time lead the horse with a new backseat passenger.

She hears the children laugh and shout from their seats in the audience. 'He's behind you!'

Sheila smiles knowing her two grandsons will be in the front row and it wouldn't be fair to disappoint them by doing what she really wants to do which is pull backwards out of the horse and run for the hills.

Gritting her teeth, she copies his movements by synchronizing their footsteps together in a haphazard trotting dance which makes the children laugh even louder.

It's the same performance they've done for the last seven years but this Christmas it is going to be different. As they finish their sequence of trotting, Sheila has her plan firmly in place.

She can hear everyone clapping and knows it is time for them to take a bow. She scrambles from the back of the costume while Ian takes her hand in his sweaty palm, and they bow from the waist. Sheila rubs the small of her back which is aching from her crouched position and grins at the children. At least they've enjoyed her performance.

As they leave the stage, he says, 'You were a little late on that last canter in the corner.'

Reaching the small changing room, she pulls the sweaty T-shirt over her head and tuts loudly.

Ian stares at her and takes a deep noisy sigh. 'What's the matter with you now?'

'Nothing,' she says and shakes her head.

She imagines his smug face at the Christmas party later with the villagers. He'll do the usual boast about their expertise and his theatrical experience. Where, in fact, he'd only had a brief walk-on part in a Midsomer Murder episode they'd filmed in the nearby village years ago. He'd stepped in when the professional actor had fallen and broke his ankle.

At last year's Christmas party, the old postmistress had asked Sheila if she always took the backseat in their lives, and she'd replied with a humorous anecdote. However, her comment had niggled away in the back of Sheila's mind ever since.

Sheila follows him out of the village hall then strides ahead of him to the party. She barges past him aiming for the mulled wine tray. Her throat is dry with the stuffy atmosphere in the horse, and she gulps at the wine. After hugs and kisses from her daughter and grandsons she munches into a mince pie.

Ian's shoulders and chest are pulled back and although Sheila can't hear his words, she knows he is bragging to the party-goers. She glares at his back and decides the time has come to make her hasty retreat.

She visualises the holdall in the hall cupboard that she packed last week and slips quietly out of the side door to leave for the Darlington Train Station.

Refugees Have Christmas Too

'But we must have our Christmas tree in the market place!' Gemma wailed.

The vicar had just said, 'Our lights and most of the decorations have been condemned by an electrician because they're so old - there's not much point having a tree if we've nothing to put on it.'

Following this news there were loud gasps and tuts from her neighbours and villagers of Haltwhistle. They'd gathered in the church hall, and she was sitting next to Ms Horsfield, the librarian. They looked at each other in horror. The meeting to discuss their Christmas festivities had just begun and Gemma had thought it would be the same as every other year.

Looking at everyone, she sighed heavily. 'So, what are we going to do?'

Gemma looked directly at their new young vicar who gave her his pleasant reassuring smile. He shrugged his shoulders. 'I'm afraid there's nothing much in the church funds to help out either.'

Ms Horsfield stood up and turned to face everyone. 'Well, we need to come up with some suggestions of how to raise the money.'

Gemma watched her neighbours nod in agreement and look at each other with blank stares.

A young woman in the front row who Gemma knew was a teaching assistant raised her hand. 'I could get the children to make handcrafted paper chains.'

This started a buzz of conversation. Two elderly ladies at the back of the room who proudly wore WI badges suggested that their group could try to repair the old garlands as best they could.

The pub landlord spoke up. 'My son works in IT – he could make some posters and we could put them in the pub, corner shop, library, and GP surgery urging everyone to give generously towards the new lights and decorations – if that would help?'

Ms Horsfield clapped her hands together. 'That's great but we need more of a substantial donation, maybe from a company? I reckon a couple of thousand should do the trick.'

The vicar sighed. 'So, tell me if I'm wrong but we don't have any businesses in Haltwhistle – do we?'

Gemma glanced at her mobile and read a message from her sister who'd started her new job in the office at the nearby chemical manufacturers. 'Hey,' Gemma said. 'How about the chemical factory?'

She watched everyone look at each other and nod.

The vicar said, 'Well, I think it's definitely worth a shot. And perhaps as a newcomer I should be the one to go with my cap-in-hand, as it were?'

Ms Horsfield offered to accompany the vicar to negotiate a bequest and Gemma smiled. 'It might just work because I figure nearly every family in Haltwhistle has someone or knows someone who works there?'

The next day, Gemma bumped into a woman leaving the corner shop with two small children. She knew it was a refugee family who had lately arrived. Through broken English and lots of smiles they managed to talk. Gemma learnt how they'd left their country with only the things they could carry.

'We had our own traditions at home for Christmas,' the Mother said wistfully. 'The children had painted wood toys, we had a small tree from the forest, home-baked goodies and lots of laughter. But here, I have no money to treat the children.'

Two weeks later at the next meeting Gemma told everyone. 'I've been talking to the Mother of a refugee family and they've absolutely nothing,' she said. 'But she told me, that at least they were safe now, which in itself, was a Christmas gift.'

Ms Horsfield stood up to get everyone's attention. 'So, our request has been a huge success - we got all of the money we'd asked for and a little more!'

Everyone began to clap, and the vicar blushed giving a little bow. 'A newspaper reporter is coming to the next meeting where the manager of the factory will hand over the money,' he said. 'It's a publicity stunt for them but at least we'll have our tree and decorations.'

The WI ladies presented the repaired garlands, and the teaching assistant displayed the paperchains. Everyone was delighted that they still had the decorations they'd known and loved for years in Haltwhistle. Memories were shared from the villagers about the students from Haltwhistle Academy who had sung carols and the Christmas party at the community centre.

Gemma sighed. 'I was just thinking about the refugee Mother and her traditional festivities at Christmas in her homeland.'

A vote was taken, and they decided their old decorations looked better than spending money on new jazzy ones.

Ms Horsfield suggested, 'So, after we've bought new lights and a tree maybe the rest of the money could go to the refugee families in the area to spend on their children?'

Everyone cheered. The vicar beamed. And Gemma wiped a tear from her cheek. 'This is what can happen when a community pulls together at Christmas.'

Printed in Great Britain
by Amazon